ELLEN POTTER

SCHOLASTIC INC.
New York Toronto London Auckland
Sydney Mexico City New Delhi Hong Kong

ISBN 978-0-545-49445-8

 Published by Scholastic Inc.,
557 Broadway, New York, NY 10012,
by arrangement with Feiwel and Friends, an imprint of Macmillan.

12 11 10 9 8 7 6 5 4 3 2 12 13 14 15 16 17/0

Printed in the U.S.A. 40

First Scholastic printing, September 2012

Book design by Patrick Collins

For Daniel, Meagan,
and Matthew Linzer

Chapter 1

There are no road signs to mark the tiny village of Limpette. It lies between two towns that you have never heard of. If you pass Ostrander's goat farm, you've gone too far.

We won't stay long in Limpette. There's not much of anything here for us, except the girl. And the girl was not much of anything either, not back then. Her name was Roo Fanshaw and she was too small for her age. She had a narrow, bony face and a tight, dissatisfied mouth. Her rusty brown hair was shoulder length, with bangs that hung over her eyes. They were green eyes. Green eyes are often very captivating, but Roo's eyes were the spent, dull green of smoke at the end of a fireworks show.

In order to see her, we need to get down on all fours

and squeeze through an opening in the vinyl apron that surrounds the bottom of her family's mobile home. It's a small opening, and we'll have more trouble getting through than Roo did. She can slip through the narrowest gaps like a ferret. Like all good thieves, she understands space. Space can be a friend or an enemy, so you should always know how much of it your body needs. Roo, being tiny, needs very little, and she feels most comfortable in cramped areas, like this one.

Duck your head. There she is. Let's begin.

With her legs pulled up and her chin on her knee, Roo listened to the sound of men's footsteps above her head. They tramped back and forth, from the living room to the bedroom beside it. She supposed they were tramping through her own bedroom too, but there was nothing of interest for them there.

The thing of interest was directly above her head. The men kept returning to that spot. She could hear their voices too, but could not make out the words. One man threw up. She heard the sound of retching and then footsteps rushing off. To the bathroom maybe?

She knew they were going to find her eventually. She considered, in an offhand way, what would happen to her when they did. In the end, she decided she didn't really care. She had been shivering badly—whether from cold or from fear, she wasn't sure. Now her body was still again. Quiet. There was nothing to do but wait.

She turned her attention to the tiny green snake that

was balanced on the knee of her tan corduroys. The light from the narrow break in the trailer's vinyl apron passed through the snake and turned it the sort of green Roo's eyes might have been, had her life been different—emerald and clear. The snake's undulating body looked so cool and smooth that Roo stuck out her tongue and licked it. Oddly, she could feel imperfections on the glass—small bumps and scuffs—that her eyes could not detect.

All around her on the icy, packed earth were dozens of tiny flowers, some made of blown glass, some trapped in Lucite domes—daisies, tiger lilies, a bouquet of pink roses, paper-thin red poppies. There was a pair of enamel earrings shaped like marigolds, large and gaudy, which she had stolen from the drugstore. She had mounded up earth and planted them by sticking their posts through the ground. Roo considered the little garden before nudging the poppies closer to the marigolds and putting the snake between them. Then she flung herself to the ground and listened to the earth. It was something she often did, checking the ground the way other girls might check the mirror. She could hear all its movements, small, fluttering sounds of life that fascinated her. Here, beneath the trailer, the sounds were stealthy, quiet stirrings of slow-moving bugs. The squeezing and shoving of ice crystals in the March thaw.

She heard a new sound, aboveground and close by. Opening her eyes, she saw the mouse a few feet away, staring at her. Very slowly, Roo stretched out her hand and wiggled her fingers toward him, happy to see him.

He edged closer to her. Hoping for food, as usual. She wished she had some. In any case, he came close enough to let her stroke his back, the fur still thick from the winter and the color of buckwheat honey.

"Stay with me, stay with me," she pleaded to him in a whisper.

But it was no good. The sound of footsteps above startled him and he was gone in a flash.

She heard the familiar suck of air as the front door to her family's home was pulled open, then the metallic clattering of someone trying to open the storm door. The latch was sticky. You had to pull the screen door toward you first in order for the latch to snap into place. The man wouldn't have known that. Roo listened as he struggled with it, trying to get out of the house, rattling the door with a few angry curses before it gave way and opened.

She held her breath. The green snake abruptly grew dark as the light from the opening was blocked by someone's leg. Roo could see the state trooper's gray pants with the thick black stripe down the sides. He was so close, Roo could have reached through the break in the apron and untied his shoes. He stood there for a moment, as still as Roo. Suddenly he shifted, moved forward. Two other legs could be seen now. These were bare and brown skinned. Lavender slippers with matted-down plush.

Mrs. Quick, the lady next door.

Roo narrowed her eyes.

"You the one I'm supposed to talk to?" Roo heard Mrs. Quick ask.

"Yes, ma'am. My name is Officer Catlin."

"I know who you are, Jason Catlin, who lives down on Myrtle Street, so don't *officer* me. Did you catch them who done this?"

"We have someone in custody, ma'am. How well did you know the family?" The state trooper sounded a little shaky. Maybe he was cold.

"Is all of them dead, then? The girl too?" Mrs. Quick's voice was whispery, like she was talking in a dark room.

"Ma'am, please. How well do you know them?" The trooper's voice was young. Roo noticed he changed to the present tense.

"I know the girl," Mrs. Quick said.

"What about the parents?"

There was a pause. Roo could see Mrs. Quick's toes punching the top of her slippers.

"Trash."

"Trash? In what way, ma'am?"

"In what *way?*" Mrs. Quick made an *nnnn* sound. Roo knew that sound. It was Mrs. Quick's sound of disgust. "They is trash in the same way trash is always trash. Their lives is a mess. Their children's lives is a mess. Then they go hanging out with other trash and this . . . this is what happens. You better tell me right now, young man." Mrs. Quick planted her legs farther apart. Roo guessed she was crossing her arms over her large chest. "What happened to the girl?"

"We don't know where she is, ma'am," the trooper admitted in a quiet voice. "When did you see her last?"

"Wasn't but a few hours ago."

"Can you say exactly?"

"After she come home from school. So maybe three forty? I seen her sitting outside her trailer, dressed in a T-shirt. A T-shirt in this weather! I told her to come in for pie. I feed her when I can. The child is *stunted*. Twelve years old and no bigger than my eight-year-old granddaughter. Roo's mother . . . oh, what the heck's the woman's name . . . Joley,"—Mrs. Quick *nnnn*'ed—"she treats Roo like a stray cat, putting her out in the cold, never dressing her proper, never feeding her proper."

Roo took the snake off her knee and placed it beside the marigold earring.

"Did she say anything about her family being in trouble? Or in danger?" the trooper asked.

"Roo? Ha! That child hardly never says nothing. She's halfway to being a savage. She just woofed down her pie, stole the snake when my back was turned, and out she went."

"She stole something?"

Roo stared at the glass snake on the ground, listening.

"Now, don't get the wrong idea. She don't steal nothing valuable. Just doodads, little this-and-thats I find at the dollar store. I leave them out for her. She wouldn't take them if I gave them to her. Too proud. Though where she gets that kind of pride, with her parents being what they are, I have no idea. So I turn my back and let her steal them. Make her feel good. Make her feel like she got something nice in her life."

A rush of blood heated Roo's face. She made a fist and held it over the snake, poised to smash it, but found that she couldn't. Instead she lunged forward toward the hole in the apron and spit. She had meant to spit on the ground, but at that moment Mrs. Quick stepped forward, and the spit landed on her bare leg. Roo watched the spit slide down Mrs. Quick's leg and slip beneath her lavender slippers, but still Mrs. Quick did not move.

"What will you do with Roo when you all find her?" Mrs. Quick asked the trooper.

"A family member has already been contacted," he said.

Roo frowned. *Family?* She had no other family. No cousins. No aunts or uncles. She supposed there might be grandparents somewhere but she didn't know them or care about them. And since they'd never bothered to see her, she guessed they didn't care about her either.

"They decent folks, Jason? These relatives of Roo's?" Mrs. Quick asked.

"I couldn't say, ma'am," the trooper admitted. There was a pause, before he added in a low voice, "I did hear they have money."

"You mean they're rich?" Mrs. Quick's voice sounded astonished.

"That's what I heard," the officer admitted.

"In that case, Officer Jason Catlin, you might want to peek under the trailer. Mind your fingers though. She bites."

Chapter 2

As it turned out, Roo had an uncle. He didn't come for her right away though. He was traveling, she was told, and no one could get in touch with him. In the meantime, Roo was placed in a foster home with a Mr. and Mrs. Burrow. She was wedged into a room with three other foster girls whom she instantly hated. They hated her right back.

She tried to stay clear of them, finding hiding places throughout the house. They hunted her down for sport, but rarely found her. One afternoon, in a brambly corner of the garden, she found a dilapidated greenhouse where Mr. Burrow started his tomato plants. Roo sat on a bag of fertilizer, watching a spider spin its web. Its tiny legs fretted and fussed with the webbing. It reminded her of the way her father's fingers looked when they picked at his guitar listlessly while waiting for something to happen: a phone call, a knock on the door. Long, elegant fingers. Fingers that seemed to be on the wrong person's hand.

Suddenly the greenhouse door was yanked open and the two older foster girls appeared. Roo looked up at them briefly, then her eyes slid back to the spider.

"Your uncle isn't coming, you know," one of the girls said. "They told him what a jerk you are, and he said, 'No, thanks, you can keep her.' "

"I don't care if he comes or not," Roo said.

They tried a different approach. "Your parents were drug dealers."

"So?"

"So . . ." The girl fumbled. "So. You'll grow up bad too. It's in the blood."

"I might," Roo said.

The girls did not know what to do with Roo. She never responded the way she should. In the end they left her alone, but in a fit of pique they padlocked the greenhouse door. It didn't matter. She watched the spider finish her web and afterward easily crawled through a loose pane of glass in the roof.

Roo's uncle did come to fetch her, although he didn't come himself. Instead he sent his personal assistant. Ms. Valentine was slim and handsome, though not young. She had dark hair, fine pale skin, and an aquiline nose. Although she was primly dressed in tweed pants, a black wool coat, and a black cardigan, she wore a peculiar purple hat that was shaped like a thimble and wrapped with a brown velvet ribbon above the brim.

She eyed Roo's Hefty bag full of clothes with distaste, before she put it up on the train's luggage shelf, shoveling it into the compartment with her fingertips. As she did, Roo slipped by her and tucked herself into the window seat.

"Don't expect a view," Ms. Valentine warned, staring down at Roo. "It's backyards and scrubby bits all the way."

She waited for Roo's face to register disappointment, but the faded green eyes stared back at her coolly.

Strange girl, Ms. Valentine thought. *She doesn't look as if she's ever shed a tear.*

Ms. Valentine removed her coat before she sat down, folding it neatly on her lap, and on top of that she placed her extraordinary hat. Then, with no jolt at all, the train moved smoothly out of the station.

"How old are you?" Ms. Valentine asked stiffly, after a time.

"Twelve."

She turned to look at Roo fully now, the first time she had done so since she'd picked her up at the Burrows' house. "That's what they told us, but you seem much too small for twelve," she pronounced. "Is there something the matter with you?"

"Is there something the matter with *you?*" Roo shot back.

"Now, there's no room for touchiness at Cough Rock, young lady," Ms. Valentine warned.

"What's that?" Roo asked. "Cough Rock."

"Your uncle's place." She glanced at Roo quickly and sighed. "You should be warned, I guess. It's an odd place. You aren't a nervous type, are you?"

Roo shook her head.

"Well, we'll find out soon enough," she said doubtfully. "The house is large, but you are not to go poking around, do you understand? Your uncle would be very angry. He has laid down rules, and we all follow them. You will too."

Ms. Valentine rubbed her thumb against her hat's ribbon. After a moment she added in a more gentle tone, "Of course, we *are* sorry about your loss. Your uncle adored your father, you know. He tells me they were very close, back when they were boys. I met your father once years ago. He was wild and foolish, but he was—" Ms. Valentine paused.

Roo looked up at her. For the first time that day she was interested in what Ms. Valentine had to say.

"I think he had a good heart. Underneath," Ms. Valentine concluded.

It was what Roo had hoped to hear. It was what she felt about him herself, though no one else seemed to share that opinion. Her father was by turns considered a drug dealer, a shady character, a loser. Still Ms. Valentine's words made her feel worse somehow.

"I was very sad to hear of his death," Ms. Valentine said. "Your mother's too, of course," she added.

"It was their own fault," Roo said simply. She turned away to stare out the dirt-flecked window.

Ms. Valentine's tidy brow furrowed at this. *Strange girl,* she thought for the second time. But now it was more of a verdict.

"And she wasn't my mother," Roo added suddenly. "She was just his girlfriend."

"Really?" Ms. Valentine turned to Roo, her voice rising with sudden interest. "You have a mother? Where is she?"

Roo shrugged.

The conductor approached and Ms. Valentine turned away from Roo to hand the man their tickets. He snapped holes in them and shoved them into the metal holder above the seats.

"What's your mother's name?" Ms. Valentine pursued after the conductor left.

Roo shrugged.

"What do you mean—?" Ms. Valentine imitated Roo's shrug and scowl. "You don't know your own mother's name?"

"She was just another girlfriend. She didn't want me. My father did. That's all I know."

They rode in silence for a while. The train was quiet, not rattly as Roo had imagined it would be. It slid along the rails, bellying from side to side, so that these two stiff creatures bumped against each other occasionally, and pretended they hadn't.

After some time, Ms. Valentine spoke again.

"I suppose you've heard all sorts of nonsense about your uncle?"

"No," Roo said.

She turned to Roo. "Well, what *have* you heard?"

"Nothing," Roo said.

"Your father must have told you something about him."

"I didn't know I had an uncle."

"Really?" Ms. Valentine gave the hat a little joggle. "Well," she said, her voice sounding more businesslike, "then here's what you *should* know about your uncle. You are not to upset him. You are not to pester him. You are not to ask him questions."

"Questions about what?" she asked.

"About anything at all," Ms. Valentine warned sharply. "He's agreed to take you in, and that's all you need to know. He feels very guilty about your father, although I don't see why he should. Your father left home at fifteen—wanted to do things his own way, so I'm told—and his father washed his hands of him, money and all. Your uncle tried to track your father many times, but he couldn't find him."

"We moved around," Roo muttered. In fact they moved every few months, whenever her father would get in trouble with the law. They had stayed in Limpette longer than any other place—nearly a year.

"Well, I hope he managed to keep you in school while he was moving you hither and thither."

"Sometimes."

"*Some*times?" Ms. Valentine exclaimed.

In fact, they had moved around so much that she often missed long stretches of school, much to her relief. She hated school. Not the books and learning part; her mind was quick enough. What she hated was being forced to be around other kids. At every new school she went to, the kids made fun of her dirty, worn-out clothes and her wild-looking hair. She defied them by letting herself grow more wild until she looked so frightening that no one would come near her. And that suited her just fine.

There was a small plastic table that was latched flat against the seat in front of her. Roo flicked the latch carelessly with her index finger, causing the table to slam down loudly. The man in front of her turned to frown at her, as did Ms. Valentine.

Roo swung her legs up and rested her sneakers on the table.

"Feet off," Ms. Valentine hissed, staring with disgust at Roo's sneakers. "People eat on that table."

It made Roo look at her feet more closely. The plastic soles of her sneakers were peeling up and the once-white tops were now gray. The bottoms of her pants were shredded from being too long and constantly stepped on. She felt Ms. Valentine's eyes on her feet too. That made her mad, so she kept her sneakers on the table.

"If you become too much trouble," Ms. Valentine cautioned, "you'll be sent back straight to the Burrows, that's a promise. It's madness for your uncle to take you on. I told him so."

She waited another moment for Roo to move her legs. When she didn't, Ms. Valentine snuffled loudly through her fine, narrow nose. Then she rummaged through her bag, making the thick charm bracelet on her wrist chime, until she retrieved a copy of *The New York Times* and a store-bought yogurt parfait with a plastic spoon. She settled back into her seat, snapped the paper open, and from then on she pretended Roo no longer existed.

That was fine with Roo. For the rest of the trip Roo watched the passing stretches of dreary brown hills and bare trees, their branches crosshatched against the cold gray sky. Occasionally they passed towns that looked much like Limpette, with their lopsided houses and scrappy backyards, until they vanished, giving way to long stretches of woods. It might have made most people feel both wistful and frightened. But for Roo, who understood things in terms of space, feeling wistful about the past and nervous about the future was too much like standing alone and exposed in acres of open field. It was unsafe. Instead she tucked her mind into a smaller thought: *What was it that her uncle did not want her to ask about?*

Roo's father and his girlfriend, Joley, had secrets, but they kept them very poorly. They fought too loudly, and all their troubles spilled out in an ugly mess. But most adults, Roo suspected, would be more careful.

Was her uncle involved in something illegal, like her

father? It seemed unlikely that a criminal would have a personal assistant. And it seemed even more unlikely that someone like Ms. Valentine would work for a criminal.

Or maybe there was something wrong with him. Maybe he had a violent temper, like Joley. At least if it was a big house, she could find places to hide.

The train turned sharply and the late afternoon sun flooded the car. Ms. Valentine shielded her face with her hat. Roo closed her eyes and slipped her hand in her jacket pocket to feel the cool smoothness of the little glass snake. It was so thin that she could have snapped it in half between her fingers.

Another possibility occurred to her then, one that struck her as by far the most interesting. Maybe her uncle was exactly like her. Maybe he simply wanted to be left alone. Roo had never understood the strange attraction people had for one another. It baffled her the way people always herded up, endlessly talking, talking. What on earth did they have to say to each other?

Roo's father liked to talk, but with him it was different. He didn't care if you spoke back. He just knew the sort of things that people liked to hear, and told it to them in his dreamy, slow way. Every so often, someone would call him charming.

"Let's see him charm the bars off his cell," Joley had said as she stood at the top of the trailer's steps and watched the police car haul him off one night. She laughed, the little metal stud in her tongue glinting off the police car's headlights. But he was back home the following day, looking tired and with a bruise on his cheekbone but otherwise no worse for it.

No matter what sort of trouble he got into, he had always managed to slip out of it. Until a few weeks ago.

Thinking about her father made Roo's chest ache. She forced her mind to collapse down again, until it was as narrow as a squint—just wide enough to numbly watch the miles and miles of dull brown views out the window. And to wonder what sort of place Cough Rock would be.

Chapter 3

They arrived in Clayton at dusk. The air was colder here. It pierced Roo's lungs and made her cough. A steady wind blew her hair into her eyes so that she had to put up her sweatshirt hood and shove her hair beneath it in order to see.

Like Limpette, Clayton was a small town but the houses here were neat and pretty. The main street was flanked by a river so vast and gray and agitated that it looked more like an ocean. Here and there chunks of ice floated upriver. They seemed to follow each other, like migrating fish.

"This way," Ms. Valentine said, and she began to walk briskly down the deserted main street. They passed souvenir shops and little eateries, some of which had signs hanging in the window saying CLOSED FOR THE SEASON.

Finally they came to a pier, empty except for one gleaming white boat wildly bucking on the waves.

Ms. Valentine walked up next to it, leaned across, and pulled it close to the pier.

"Step in," she told Roo.

"Why?" Roo asked, eyeing the boat as it jumped about on the waves.

"Because unless you have wings under your sweatshirt, there's no other way. Cough Rock is an island."

"I don't like water. I can't swim," Roo told her, staring warily at the tossing boat.

"She's a Boston Whaler. She won't sink. In you go."

After a moment's hesitation, Roo stepped in the boat and immediately stumbled forward as it pitched, but caught herself before her chin slammed against the console. Meanwhile Ms. Valentine deftly untied the mooring ropes and hopped in. She pushed a button on the console, pushed forward a black lever, and turned the ignition. The motor burbled, then the boat sped away from the pier and into the open river.

The water looked thick, like an expanse of angry gray muscle. It shoved at the boat mercilessly, tossing them about, making Roo feel helpless and angry. Ms. Valentine, on the other hand, seemed completely untroubled. She sat very upright, just as though she were still riding the train, and steered lightly with only two fingers on the wheel.

There were islands everywhere, some quite small and others large enough to hold several houses. And not just houses; these were mansions, the sort that Roo had only ever seen on television, half hidden by a tangle of winter branches and evergreens. They looked as deserted as the town had.

Above them, a slender shadow suddenly appeared. Roo looked up to see a large bird, its neck as long as a swan's, awkwardly pushing through the dimming sky. The bird followed them for a while. Roo twisted her head to get a better look at it, but it seemed to dodge her glances, moving over the top of the boat where the canopy blocked her view until finally, with a rough croak, it flew away.

"A heron," Ms. Valentine told her. "Don't worry, you'll see plenty more." Then added, more to herself, "Though it's odd to see them this time of year."

Finally, they turned toward one of the islands. It rose up high out of the water, its banks a tall ledge of sharp-edged rocks. Above the rocks the land leveled out. Occupying most of the island was a huge stone building. Despite its size, it was plain, with no adornments except for a deck that wrapped around its lower floor. It didn't look like someone's house, Roo thought. It looked like an old school or a factory. Someplace where no one would want to live.

Ms. Valentine circled the island and pulled the throttle. The boat slowed, and Ms. Valentine guided it toward a tremendous stone arch that served as a gateway into the island's small lagoon. Because of the darkening sky, they were nearly beneath the arch when Roo could finally make out the words carved across the top of it: ST. THERESA'S CHILDREN'S HOSPITAL. Her muscles tightened.

Where had she been taken?

Once in the lagoon, Ms. Valentine pulled up alongside the pier and cut the motor.

"This is it," Ms. Valentine said. "Out you go."

"No."

Ms. Valentine gazed down at Roo, and her slender nostrils dilated with indignation. Her purple hat was in her hand, the wind curling its rim up.

"No *what*?"

"I'm not going," Roo said.

"Don't be ridiculous. You have nowhere else to go," she said, stepping out onto the pier.

"You lied to me," Roo spat back at her.

"Are you completely mad?" Ms. Valentine looked appalled.

"I'm supposed to be going to my uncle's, not a children's hospital," Roo said.

"What on earth are you talking about?" Ms. Valentine stared at Roo with angry befuddlement before she finally fluttered her eyes skyward and said, "The arch."

Reaching into the back of the boat, she heaved up Roo's Hefty bag, then said, not unkindly, "It's an old sign, Roo. This hasn't been a children's hospital in over sixty years."

Roo stared up at the windows of the house. There were many of them but no children in sight. The island was silent too. If anything, it seemed as abandoned as the other islands.

Roo stood and climbed out of the boat awkwardly, then followed Ms. Valentine up a stone walkway. The walkway cut through the island's sparse lawn, still snow flecked, up red-veined granite stairs and through a massive set of oak doors.

In the entrance foyer, Ms. Valentine paused to remove her purple hat and place it on a brass peg on the wall before she led Roo into a large lobby, past a staircase, and then down a dark hallway. There were many rooms off the hallway. All of them, Roo noticed, were on the left-hand side. Most doors were shut but some were open, and in these Roo spied shadowy furnishings and large windows covered with heavy drapes. The walls along the hallway seemed strangely lumpy. Her fingers swiped at them surreptitiously but it was too dark in the hallway to see what they were.

Finally, Ms. Valentine stopped in front of a closed door. She gave Roo a look of sharp appraisal before extending one disdainful forefinger, intent on pushing aside Roo's overgrown bangs. But Roo knocked her hand out of the way before she could.

"Fine, look like a beast then," Ms. Valentine said. She gave the door a quiet rap with a flourish of her knuckles. After a pause, Roo heard a response from within.

"Yes. What is it?"

Roo listened hard to his voice. It sounded rough and tense. Nothing like her father's easy crooning.

"Your niece has arrived, Mr. Fanshaw," Ms. Valentine called.

There was no reply. Roo glanced up at Ms. Valentine to see what was wrong, but she seemed untroubled by the silence.

"Roo is right here, Mr. Fanshaw. Shall we come in?" Ms. Valentine persisted, polite but determined.

"No." The response came. "Not now. I'll see her later."

Ms. Valentine stood at the door a moment longer, then sniffed and turned.

"Just as well," she said to Roo. "You should have a bath first and fresh clothes. Come, I'll show you your room."

"Why wouldn't he see me?" Roo asked as they walked back up the hallway toward the lobby.

"There's no need to get offended," Ms. Valentine said.

"I'm not. I just want to know why."

After a moment Ms. Valentine said, "Your uncle has always been a private person. Circumstances have made him . . . more so.

"This is the west wing of the house," Ms. Valentine told her as they began to climb the staircase in the lobby. "The upstairs renovations are still underway." There was a dry tone in her voice that made Roo think that this wasn't exactly the truth.

On the second-floor landing, Ms. Valentine's low heels clicked briskly across the polished wooden hallway floor and turned into the first room on the left.

It was a massive bedroom, easily twice the size of the living room in the old trailer. There were very few furnishings—just a bed and a plain wardrobe—which made the room seem even larger. By the window was a recessed window seat with a view of the river.

"It's nothing fancy but better than you're used to," Ms. Valentine said. "We've bought some clothes for you. They're in the wardrobe, though I'm sure they won't fit well. We didn't expect you to be so small." She opened a door by the wardrobe. "Bathroom." She closed the door again. "Down the hall are some other rooms that have never been used. You are free to poke around. The east wing, however, is strictly off-limits. That's one rule you do not want to break in this house."

And with that, Ms. Valentine *click-clacked* out of the room and back down the hall.

It didn't take Roo long to see that there was no good place to hide in this room. The bed was too low-slung. There was a wardrobe, but it was indeed full of clothes and difficult to close from the inside. It all made her feel so horribly trapped, like a wild young fox that someone had snatched from the woods, dropped into a strange cavernous room, and then left all alone.

Roo collapsed on the floor and began to cry. Her sobs were awful—the agonized tears of old sorrows and sorrows too new and raw to understand. She jammed her wrist in her mouth and bit it to make herself stop, but she succeeded only in turning her sobs into a muffled wail. She cried and cried until, quite suddenly, the tears stopped. She lifted her head. Through bleary eyes she gazed around as if trying to remember where she was.

Her fingers slipped into her jacket pocket and closed around the green snake. Snorting back mucus, she shook her bangs out of her eyes, and went out into the hallway. She paused to listen. There was only silence.

Cautiously, she started up the hall, noting things along the way. The right side of the wall was covered with fresh Sheetrock, the screw heads still showing. The other side of the hall was painted a soft blue. There was an open door just past her bedroom. Peering in she found a smallish room with no furniture. The wooden floors were stripped down, dull, and pale and waiting for varnish. Up ahead, the hallway took a sharp turn. Everything here was different, as though she suddenly had stepped into another building. The right-hand walls still had the bare Sheetrock but the walls on the left were a liver color, peeling and grimy. The floors didn't gleam as they did down the other hallway. Here they were scarred and worn, beneath a ceiling that dripped bare lightbulbs. The temperature had plummeted too, as though not even the heat wanted to linger here.

Was this the east wing, where she was forbidden to go?

She stood very still for a moment, listening. No, not listening exactly. It was more like sensing. She tested places in this way. In some places the air felt very full. These places smothered her; too many people came and went. She preferred the places where the air felt wispy, where everything passed through lightly and carefully. The crawlspace beneath the trailer had been like that. The dirt floor showed the occasional pinprick footprints of mice or the smudged ripple of a snake, but that was all.

This place, though, was like nothing she'd ever experienced before. The air was dead, as if all living smells had been deliberately scoured away.

She pushed on the doorknob of the first room she came to. This room was full of ancient, wicker-backed wheelchairs. Heaped on one of the wheelchairs were several white smocks, yellowed with age. There were three other doors in the hallway, one an old bathroom with its plumbing ripped out, and the other a room so tiny it could only have been some sort of closet.

The last door in the hallway wouldn't open, but Roo could feel that it wanted to. She leaned all her weight against it. It budged a little but still would not give way. Holding the knob, she drew back and gave the door a sharp kick. With a *crack* the door flew open, and an acrid smell hit Roo's nostrils, layered with the parched odor of dust. The room was large and painted the same awful color of the hallway, but there were curtains with a childish pattern of yellow and red rocking horses, faded where the sun hit it in the center but still bright along the edges. Lining two walls were a half-dozen iron bed frames, painted white, with no mattresses. The beds were small. Child-size. There was a washbasin in one corner, and a beadboard cabinet against the far wall. That was all. Except for the smell.

This must have once been part of the children's hospital, she thought.

She walked over to one of the beds and ran her hand along the cold metal headboard. She sat on the bare springs and bounced a few times, listening to the squeak and breathing in the smell of rust. From this perch her sharp eyes slid across the room, studying every inch. She had learned that if you concentrated on anything long enough, the hidden things would show themselves. Sure enough, at the far end of the room, beneath a corner bed, she spotted a floorboard that did not lie flush with the floor. Hopping off the bed she went over to examine it. It was wedged tightly in place, though a sliver of its edges showed above the level of the floor. Roo pried at it with her narrow fingers, patiently nudging and pulling until the board came up in her hands. A puff of dust came up with it and in the space below was a wooden box painted a faded mustard color. She pulled it out and placed it in front of her. There was a small iron lock with a catch, which she flicked up with her pinky. Opening the lid, she found inside a flashlight, a ring, and an opened pack of Juicy Fruit gum. The flashlight was ancient looking, with a silver body and brass fittings on either end. She flipped the flashlight's switch but the batteries were dead. The ring was nice though. A thin silver band with two tiny silver hearts fused together. She picked up the gum. The package was old-fashioned looking, with green and white stripes. She pulled out a stick of the gum. It was rock hard and wrapped in the same green-and-white paper, but instead of foil the gum itself was covered with a red wax paper. She put the flashlight and the gum back in the box, but slipped the ring on her finger. The feel of it steadied her and gave her more confidence. She shut the box's lid and replaced it in its hiding place.

A sudden sound made Roo shove the floorboard back into place and jump to her feet. If Ms. Valentine found her here, in what she suspected was the forbidden east wing, she would be furious. Maybe Ms. Valentine would even go through with her threat to send Roo back to the Burrows. She felt the urge to hide, but she fought it with cool common sense.

What do I care if she sends me back there? One place is as good as another.

She waited, watching the open door to see if someone would pass by, but no one did. Crossing the room, Roo peered around the door into the hallway. There was no one in sight, but the next moment she heard the sound again. It was a droning noise, and at first Roo thought it might be some sort of motor. But as she listened she could hear that it rose and fell in pitch and volume at irregular intervals. It was a human sound, absolutely. The sound of humming. She listened for a tune, but there wasn't one. The voice hummed on and on, joyless, as if someone were forcing it to hum.

Roo pressed her ear against the wall at the far end of the room. The sound was not there, not quite. Instead, it seemed to fill the air around her, to be everywhere and nowhere. Then, very suddenly, it stopped.

"Is someone in there?" she whispered to the wall,

and put her ear against it again. Nothing. She knocked at the Sheetrock.

"Who's there?" she asked more loudly.

She was answered by a scream, so loud and piercing that Roo instantly crouched down, muscles clenched, like an animal readying itself to escape or, if necessary, fight.

Chapter 4

The scream quickly changed to an outburst of laughter, loud and unrestrained. Roo looked up to see a remarkably pretty girl staring down at her with surprised delight. She was quite tall and broad shouldered, and looked to be twenty or so. Her sleek black hair was pulled back in a long braid and she wore a white cable sweater over jeans.

"Stop it!" Roo demanded, standing up. "Stop laughing at me!"

The girl did stop laughing, disarmingly fast. Her eyes grew wide as she gazed at Roo. "Ooo, so there it is," she said.

When she didn't explain herself, Roo was forced to ask, "There is *what*?"

The girl laughed again.

Roo lunged at her then, her hands stretched out, intent on slapping or shoving, but the girl caught Roo around her middle. She tipped her down so that she was parallel to the floor and held her like that as Roo kicked and screamed in a wild fit of anger. Remarkably, not a single kick landed.

"There's the Fanshaw pride in you. Ms. Valentine said she didn't see a single speck of it, but I guess she didn't get you mad enough."

"Let go!" Roo screeched.

"First calm down."

"Let go!"

"Calm down."

That infuriated Roo even more and she bellowed at the top of her lungs and flailed about so violently that this time she did manage a sharp jab of her elbow into the girl's ribs.

The girl pulled in her breath so suddenly that Roo paused in satisfaction. But then the girl said in a reasonably cheery tone, "Is that the best you can do?"

Roo tried to do better, but the girl was strong and fast. She swiftly adjusted her hold. Now Roo's arms and legs were held so fast that she could not move them at all. She frantically tried to squirm out of the girl's grip but she only managed to paddle her feet and twist her head about.

"Tsss, tsss," the girl said quietly. Her mouth was so close to Roo's head that Roo could feel the warmth of her breath against her scalp. It was strangely pleasant. In

another second Roo would remember to be angry again, but the girl let go right before that happened. Free, Roo jumped to her feet and backed herself up against the wall, staring at the girl.

"Well, that was fun," the girl said, adjusting her sweater. "I'm Violet."

She waited, but when Roo didn't respond, Violet answered for her. "Hi, Violet. I'm Roo."

Roo's eyes were fixed on Violet, the way a wild cat watches a person who is cooing to it—steady and interested but exceedingly cautious.

"If you keep staring at me like that, I'm going to laugh again," Violet warned. "And then we'll have to start all over."

Roo looked away.

"Thank you. And just so you know, I wasn't laughing at *you*—not the first time anyway. I was laughing because you scared the you-know-what-skees out of me. I thought you were the Yellow Girl. So...Ms. Valentine says I'm supposed to make sure you clean yourself up."

"That's my business, not hers."

Violet cocked her head to the side and looked Roo up and down. "You know who you remind me of? My aunt Fiona. Last spring she rowed out of Donkey Island with a backpack full of beer and a five-pound bag of cheese curd, then climbed up to an old osprey nest on top of a navigational marker. She sat there for days and days, poor Fiona, looking just like a skinny old bird sitting on her eggs. Wouldn't come down, though we all begged and yelled and threatened from our boats. She said it was her business where she sat, and if the osprey didn't mind, neither should we. She lasted a good week until she rolled over in her sleep and fell straight into the river. Poor old thing floated like a dried-out leaf, still sound asleep, and where do you think she washed up? Right back on Donkey Island, not twenty yards from her house. How's that for luck?"

Roo's jaw twitched. "Is that true?"

"Of course."

"She sounds crazy."

"There's all brands of crazy," Violet answered, raising her eyebrows. "Personally, I don't give a baked bean if you want to go around looking like something drug out of a swamp, but I like my job and I need it. I'm not going to lie to you, Roo. I'll haul you into the shower and hose you off with your clothes still on, if I have to."

Had the threat come from Ms. Valentine, Roo might have challenged it. In any case, she would have kicked and screamed and made sure that Ms. Valentine took that shower right along with her. But with this girl . . . Roo could imagine her howling with laughter as she wrestled Roo into the shower. And that would be unbearable.

In the large white-and-coral-tiled bathroom Roo stripped down. Her skin puckered up instantly from the cold. She took a furtive glance at herself in the mirror above the sink—bony, narrow shoulders. A hard boy's chest. She lifted her eyes to see her face, and stared back at herself suspiciously. She didn't wonder if she were pretty or not—she knew that she wasn't. She shook her bangs to one side. In her reflection she saw what she always saw: the downcast chin, the angry, caged-looking eyes. Her reflection shouted back at her: *This is what you are! It's in the cells of your body, it's in the coils of your brain!*

She looked away. On the sink was a dish of round pastel-colored candies that turned out to be soap. She picked them up, one at a time, and smelled each one. The smells were odd, flowery but not like any flowers she knew. She chose a yellow one and took it into the shower. The water was good and hot, not like the tepid trickle of the trailer's shower. She showered quickly, rubbing the hard little ball of soap along the back of her neck and in her armpits, then sloshing a handful of shampoo through her hair. When she came out of the bathroom, wrapped in the bathrobe that had been left for her, she found Violet carrying in a tray of food.

"Well, that's an improvement," Violet said as she looked Roo up and down. She placed the tray of food down on the window seat.

"Nothing fancy," Violet said. "Just chicken and salt potatoes. You can leave the tray, I'll get it tomorrow."

She started to leave but Roo blurted out, "Don't go."

Later Roo wondered why she had said it. She had never in her life wanted company. And if Violet had hesitated for even a second, Roo would have taken it back.

"All right," Violet said gamely, and she plunked herself down on Roo's bed. She leaned back against the headboard and watched as Roo curled into the window seat. Violet was such a big, strong, capable-looking girl that people often mistook her for a beautiful brute; but during quiet moments, like right now, her features were subtle and thoughtful.

Roo picked up a salt potato in her fingers and felt the delicate skin tear as she bit into it. It was good, and she was hungry, so she took a few more bites before pausing to ask Violet, "Are you going to tell Ms. Valentine that I was in the east wing?"

Violet tipped her head to one side and frowned. "When were you in the east wing?"

"Just now. Back there."

"You mean back in the old girls' dormitory? No, no, no." Violet smiled, the worry leaving her face instantly. "That's not the east wing. That's the old part of the west wing."

"Who lives in the west wing?" Roo asked, thinking of the humming sound.

Violet shrugged. "You. That's all. No one's lived in the west wing for years. This whole house used to be a tuberculosis sanitarium for children, oh, ages and ages ago. That's why us locals call it Cough Rock. It had a more official name, of course, but no one ever remembers it. The girls' dormitory was in this wing—that's the last room down with all the beds—and the boys' was in the east wing. After the hospital closed down, the place stood empty, right up until Mr. Fanshaw bought it. The Fanshaws had a house on Scotch Pine Island—it's where your father spent his summers when he was a kid—but your uncle sold that about ten years ago and bought Cough Rock. It seems like a funny choice, but your uncle does things his own way."

Roo picked at the skin of a chicken leg, considering this. "What's he like, my uncle?"

Violet raised her eyebrows and shrugged. "We don't see him very much. He travels." She stopped talking abruptly, though it seemed like she would say more. Roo took this in. She turned back to her food, chewing and thinking.

"I heard someone humming when I was in the hallway," Roo said.

"Humming?" Violet smiled a little. "Well, this house has got creaky old bones. It makes all kinds of noises, I guess."

"It was a person," Roo insisted.

"Maybe Ms. Valentine was humming," Violet said falteringly.

Roo could not imagine Ms. Valentine humming. And anyway the voice sounded lighter, younger.

"You said something about a Yellow Girl," Roo said. "Who is that?"

Violet widened her eyes. "Do you like ghost stories?"

"I don't know," Roo answered honestly.

"Let's find out." Violet leaned forward, clasped her hands together in her lap and gazed intently at Roo. "Years ago, when Mr. Fanshaw first started renovations on the house, he hired some contractors from Clayton.

Soon after they started work, the men began to see a little girl, walking through the hallway, wrapped in a yellow sheet. The girl would look right at them, her eyes going all wide, and she'd whisper, "Shoot." Then she'd vanish right in front of their eyes. The men thought that someone must have shot the girl, but when one of them told this story to his great-uncle, who had been alive when the sanitarium was still open, the old man shook his head. 'That child wasn't talking about guns. She was talking about the *chute*.' According to the old man, the sanitarium wasn't very good about keeping their patients alive. When one of the poor little things died, the nurses would wrap them up in a yellow sheet and send them down a secret chute. The chute led to the basement, and from there the sanitarium workers would take the body on a boat back to the mainland to be buried. This way they wouldn't upset the other patients and were able to keep the deaths quiet."

"That's awful." Roo looked away, out the window. Far below, the water was black now, except for filaments of moonlight clinging to the low crests.

"I'm a dope!" Violet cried. "Here I am, talking about ghosts after everything you've been through. Ignore me! All us folks from Donkey Island are the most superstitious people you'll ever meet. Don't believe a thing that comes out of our mouths. Of course, ghosts are nonsense. You don't believe in them, do you?"

"Of course not," Roo said irritably. And she didn't, which made the humming all the more curious.

Chapter 5

The following day, the entire household seemed to have forgotten that Roo existed. That suited her perfectly. The first thing she did was to hurry down the hall in bare feet, still dressed in her pajamas, to listen for the humming. She waited for a while, sitting on the cold hallway floor, her arms wrapped around her legs to keep the chill off them. The only sound was the hiss of the waves outside. The silence in the house had an unnatural quality, as though everything were holding its breath, waiting. It reminded Roo of the silence right before the gunshots cracked above her head at their trailer. She fought an urge to flee and kept herself rooted, just as she had underneath the trailer. Waiting. Listening. But the house remained silent and still.

Back in her room she opened the wardrobe and

fingered the clothes they had bought for her. The material was softer and thicker than she was used to. But Ms. Valentine was right; they were too big for her. She put on her old corduroys and a T-shirt from her Hefty bag, pulled her hooded sweatshirt over that, and went downstairs.

The first floor was as silent as the second, though the large windows in some of the rooms flooded the hallway with light and made the place seem less gloomy. Idly, Roo walked across the tiled floor, letting her fingers trail across the wall. Now she could see why the wall had seemed so lumpy the day before. Carved into the mahogany wainscoting were blooms of flowers. They trellised across the wall, huge and tropical looking. Hidden within the petals and crawling along the stem were tiny insects, their wings as thin as paper. Roo touched these very lightly, marveling at the hair-thin veins and the furled edges of wings. Farther up the hallway, she discovered the face of a carved monkey peering out from between a snarl of large leaves; its wide eyes stared back at her. She let her finger slip into its slightly open mouth and she felt the pinprick of tiny sharp teeth against her finger, poised to bite. She laughed at it, then stopped quickly when she heard a man's voice from farther up the hall.

"Dr. Oulette?"

That's my uncle, Roo thought.

She felt a jumble of curiosity and nervousness, though she could not understand why she should be afraid. She waited another minute, then stealthily crept along the hallway toward the room that Ms. Valentine had knocked on the day before. The door was open now. Roo peered around the door frame. It was a huge room, paneled with dark wood, its high ceiling braced with thick timber beams. Opposite the door was a large window trimmed with stained glass, giving a fine view of the stormy, gray seaway. In the center of the room was a large pool table. The green baize top was almost completely covered with maps. The maps looked as if they were photos of treetops, taken from a plane, and it was here Roo's uncle Emmett stood, with his back to Roo, studying the maps.

He was tall and slim, dressed in loose tan trousers and a silky cream-colored shirt. He should have appeared elegant, but instead he looked frail. The wrists that poked out of his sleeves were too narrow and bony for a grown man. As he stared down at the map, the fingers of his right hand rested lightly on the edge of the pool table, while the other hand was in his pocket. Roo watched him for several minutes. He did not move the entire time, not the slightest bit.

He knows how to be still. Like me.

His head swiveled toward the door, quickly, as though he had just then felt her presence. When she saw him, her eyes went wide. In front of her stood her own father, miraculously alive again. Had his murder been a lie? Or was this . . . a ghost? No, that was impossible. She wanted to run to him, to fling her arms around him and press her face into his chest. But then she noticed his eyes—flat and hard looking. They were nothing like her father's eyes. He gazed down at her, frowning absently, as though she were a disturbing thought that had suddenly popped into his head.

"I'm Roo," she said.

"Who else could you possibly be?" he replied coldly.

Now that she looked at him more carefully, she could see the differences. The thin nose was not as short as her father's. The lips more precise. He looked displeased as he took in her old sweatshirt and the frayed corduroys.

"Didn't Ms. Valentine buy you new clothes?" he asked.

"I like my own," Roo replied, her voice matching his in coldness.

He looked at her sharply, as though she had suddenly come into focus for him. "Your father was stubborn too. Much good it did him." He paused, still staring at her circumspectly, then said, "Do you miss him?" He asked this in a peculiarly unemotional way, like a doctor might poke at a wound and say, "Does this hurt?"

It made Roo angry, and she answered defiantly, "No." But her voice sounded odd. Her throat had tightened, and she realized with horror that she was a hairsbreadth away from tears.

Her uncle noticed. He sighed. His face softened, and suddenly Roo saw her father again, the likeness shocking. Mesmerizing.

"I hope you'll be happy here, Roo," he said. "If there's anything you need, you can ask Ms. Valentine."

Then he abruptly turned back to his maps. Roo stayed

where she was, staring at him. She didn't think she liked him. And he didn't seem to like her very much either. Yet she wanted him to turn around again, to relive the sensation of her father being in front of her, still alive.

Turn around, turn around . . . she willed him in her thoughts. But no, he was lost in the maps' green wilderness once again. He was done with her.

She retreated down the hallway until she found herself in the entrance lobby. Pushing open the massive front door, she stepped outside onto the cobblestone promenade. A light rain was falling, nudged this way and that by a fitful wind. Roo made her way down the granite steps toward a stretch of lawn mottled with thin patches of snow. She cut across it, past a semicircular patio, and headed toward the tiny lagoon where the moored Boston Whaler was now bobbing lightly. The wind blew more gently here, bringing with it a tangy odor of fish and cold fog. Following the path around the lagoon, she walked over the small footbridge that led to the stone archway. Here, she climbed out onto the great rocks that hemmed the edges of the island. The stones were splattered with gull droppings, but she found a clean spot and sat down.

The movement of the river was dizzying at first. The slate gray water rushed past, twisting and hissing like a tangle of frantic snakes. If you watched one spot you thought the water was rushing north, but if you shifted your glance it seemed as if it were heading east. After a few minutes Roo felt as though she were the one who was moving, and she had to take her eyes off the current to keep from feeling wobbly.

From this perch, she could see several of the other islands rising out of the restless St. Lawrence. Some had simple cottages on them, but many others had majestic houses with landscaped lawns, still winter dull and speckled with snow, sloping down toward the water. Roo had never seen anything like it. In Limpette, the fanciest building was the library, but its bricks were grimy and the front columns were peeling and listing to the right. These homes were by far the grandest she had ever seen. Yet, they all seemed deserted. No people, no boats. The only movement came from the tops of the pines as they shuddered in the wind.

The burr of a motor sliced through the river's hiss. A small boat with a bright green hull and a white canopy curled around the island and was now heading straight for the stone arch entry. Roo stiffened and hurried to her feet, intent on hiding, but it was too late. The men in the boat had spotted her. There were two of them. The older man, with graying hair and glasses, was at the wheel. He raised his hand to her in greeting. Sitting in the passenger seat was a peculiar-looking younger man dressed in a black suit jacket. He had blond hair, as thick as a lion's mane, and he stared at Roo steadily as the boat pulled through the arch and into the lagoon.

"Can it be? Is it? The famous Roo Fanshaw!" the older man called heartily to Roo as he climbed out of the boat, carrying a stack of envelopes.

This took Roo aback. How did he know who she was? She stared suspiciously at the man without saying a word. He approached her, holding out his hand, but when she didn't step forward to take it, he withdrew it and smiled quizzically.

"A shy one? Well, that's all right. Violet's mouthy enough for twenty Roo Fanshaws. I'm Simon LaShomb, the island mail carrier. Want to run this in for your uncle?" He handed Roo the stack of envelopes, bound by a rubber band, and a small padded envelope marked FRAGILE.

The man with the blond hair was standing behind the mailman, listening and watching Roo intently. Now he stepped forward rigidly. The movement made the mailman's mouth flicker briefly with displeasure.

"And who is the young lady?" the blond man asked, his eyes never leaving Roo's face. He was a short, square-shaped man with skin too olive colored for his blond hair. His cheeks were thick and oily.

"Better shake a leg, Doc." The mail carrier's voice suddenly turned curt. "The weather is only going to get nastier as the day goes on."

"Weather doesn't bother me," the blond man said evenly.

It certainly didn't seem to. While the mail carrier was wearing a nylon winter jacket, the blond man's jacket was thin, and beneath it he wore a white button-down shirt, with the top buttons undone.

"Maybe not, but it's Valentine who'll be shuttling you

back to Clayton, and I'm sure she doesn't want to get caught in a storm," Simon replied gruffly.

The blond man said nothing. He stared back at the mail carrier with a half smile on his lips, waiting until the mailman's shoulders shifted uneasily, before saying very pompously, "Thank you for the ride, kind sir." He bowed with a flourish then started up the path toward the house.

Simon LaShomb clearly found the man offensive, but he also seemed baffled by him. He watched the man's retreating back for a few moments, then he shook his head once, to himself.

"Who is that?" Roo asked.

"What? That guy? Ehh. Oulette. He's your uncle's doctor."

"Is my uncle sick?" Roo asked.

Simon's eyes flickered to the house, then back at Roo. He shrugged. "Couldn't say."

You won't *say,* Roo thought, watching the man's face carefully.

"So what do you think of island life so far?" Simon asked her, his voice more cheerful now.

"I don't like it," Roo said.

"No?" He looked surprised. But then he added, "Well, I guess it is lonely here this time of year. There's some of us year-rounders on Donkey Island, but you can't see Donkey from Cough Rock, and all the houses around here are shut up until summer. It feels like you're the only person on the planet, doesn't it? Well, when the weather turns, Violet can take you over to Donkey and find you a mess of summer kids to play with."

"I don't care about being alone," Roo said.

Simon looked pleased at this. "Well, seems like you're already a River Rat."

"What's that?"

"It's the sort of person who doesn't like a lot of jibber-jabber. The river is company enough."

"But I don't like the river," Roo said, looking out at the agitated waves.

"You don't *trust* the river," Simon said. "And you shouldn't. You don't know her yet and she doesn't know you. But you got River Rat in your DNA—your grandfather was one. He knew every musky hole for miles around. Your father was a River Rat too. He was always out on the river, trolling between the islands. That kid knew how to handle a skiff before he could ride a bike."

This interested Roo. She had only ever seen her father in a boat once, when he took her fishing on a large pond hidden up in the hills. They had stayed for hours. But what she remembered best about the trip was that it was the first time he told her the story about *Pendragon,* the flying boat. It was a red-and-yellow boat captained by a boy named Vincent, who piloted it above the treetops and through the sky. Every so often Vincent would anchor his sky boat on a rain cloud. Then he would parachute down to earth, always landing in the middle of an impossibly dangerous situation. Roo had loved the story about *Pendragon,* and whenever she had trouble sleeping, she would beg her father for a new installment about the flying boat.

"Now, your uncle in there"—Simon nodded toward the house—"he never took to the water. Afraid of it, he says so himself. He doesn't even own a boat; he has Ms. Valentine shuttle him around in hers." There was a hint of disapproval in his voice.

"Then why does he stay here?" Roo asked.

Simon hesitated, his expression suddenly turning cautious. "I guess he has his reasons," he replied. "Remember to give Valentine the mail. She won't be expecting it. I generally bring the mail to the post office on Choke Cherry Island and Valentine fetches it, but when the weather's nasty I sometimes pop by. Saves her a trip." He held out his hand again "So long, Roo Fanshaw."

This time she gave it a quick, reserved shake.

The sky was already darkening as Simon's boat pulled out of the lagoon, spun to the right, and tore off. Its wake rolled back toward the island and thrashed against the rocks for a moment or two before quieting. The water was changing color too. It was now a slick black-gray, the color of wet stone. Here and there an ice floe drifted past slowly. The river had suddenly calmed, yet Roo could feel it gathering itself together, forming something new and spiteful. It reminded her of how the girls at the Burrows' house conferred while standing a few yards away, quietly plotting some fresh torment for Roo.

From the west, a large bird appeared in the sky, its neck bent, its long body rising and dipping. A heron. Beneath the heron, drifting on the river, was a large ice floe with a curious dark shape on top of it. Roo fixed her eyes on the shadowy hump, perplexed. The floe skimmed the edge of the island closest to Cough Rock, an oval island with a neat terraced lawn that led up to a magnificent olive-green house. When the ice floe came close to the island, a black figure leapt off the ice and onto land.

Even from a distance, Roo could see that the figure was a boy. He stood on the bank for a moment, looking around. Then he grew perfectly still. It seemed to Roo that he was staring right at her, though at this distance she couldn't be certain. The boy turned abruptly and bounded up the terraced lawn, climbing the ledges rather than the stairs, and disappeared around the backside of the house.

Roo hurried back over the footbridge, skirted the lagoon, and ran around the edge of the island, trying to catch another glimpse of the boy. At first she saw nothing. But after a few seconds she spotted him again. Astonishingly, he was now standing on one of the lower roofs of the house. Suddenly he raised one arm. Was he waving to her?

The very next minute, the water darkened and became opaque. The sky seemed to drop closer to the earth, as though the river had yanked it down. A torrent of fine icy rain began to lash at the ground and peck at Roo's face. She shoved the mail beneath her shirt and pulled up her sweatshirt's hood, but the thin cotton was already soaked through. Squinting through the curtain of rain, she watched the shadowy form on the roof. Suddenly, the wind changed directions, as though someone had summoned it. It drove into her face so violently that it felt like an assault, forcing her to run. Roo refused. She turned her back to the wind, twisting her head to keep her eyes on the boy. The river grew frantic, crashing against the island's banks. Then the wind whipped around yet again, even more fiercely now, and this time Roo surrendered, running back to the house while the river thrashed and hissed triumphantly at her back.

Chapter 6

Roo burst through the door, very nearly colliding with Ms. Valentine, who was heading out, dressed in a long black raincoat and a leopard-spotted, brimmed rain hat tied under her chin. Her hand flew to her midsection in surprise. But in a blink she composed herself, taking in Roo's dripping hair and sodden clothing.

"If you are hell-bent in playing outside in bad weather, no one here will stop you. But when you get sick, there'll be no one to take care of you either."

"I won't get sick," Roo said. "I've never been sick in my life."

"This house was built for sick people," Ms. Valentine warned. "People don't tend to stay healthy here for very long." Her eyes lowered suddenly and stared at Roo's hand, which was cradling the mail beneath her sweatshirt.

"Where did you get that ring?" she asked suspiciously. "I don't remember you wearing it before."

Roo looked at the thin silver ring that she had pilfered from the girls' dormitory and then lied without any hesitation. "My father gave it to me for my twelfth birthday."

"Hmm." Ms. Valentine's lips pressed together skeptically. "And what have you got under your shirt? You look like you're hiding something."

With a deft flick of her fingers, Roo tucked the padded envelope into her waistband while she extracted the stack of envelopes from beneath her sweatshirt.

"The mailman came," she said, handing the stack to Ms. Valentine.

Ms. Valentine took the letters and quickly shuffled through them. Her expression lost some of its harshness, perhaps because now she did not have to run out for the mail in the bad weather.

"Go upstairs, Roo. Change into dry clothes. And don't play in the rain." Then Ms. Valentine started back toward the other end of the house, untying her rain hat as she went.

But Roo didn't go upstairs, not right away. She waited until Ms. Valentine had disappeared across the lobby and through a small threshold at the far end of it. Roo followed, waiting until she was sure Ms. Valentine was well ahead of her. Passing through the vaulted threshold, Roo found herself in a short foyer that led to yet another lobby, this one far larger than the first. Here, the ceiling was so tall, Roo had to tilt her head back to see it. Covering the walls were dozens of masks, some very wild looking, made from woven fibers and strung with seeds. Others were carved out of wood or gourds, with faces that peered out with alert round eyes, as though she had just startled them. One mask had a curled tongue that stuck out of its mouth.

Opposite the front door was a staircase, this one much wider and grander than the other. Its banister was carved and it twisted up and around to the second floor. Roo thought she could hear voices coming from above, so she ducked into a corridor off the lobby. There were many doors along the corridor, every one of them shut. Roo tried them all. There was a cozy-looking parlor in one, with a fireplace and two plush maroon armchairs facing each other across a little round table. In another was a tremendously long dining table with a dozen high-backed chairs poised around it. There was even what looked to be a ballroom, with a piano in the corner and wide windows that overlooked the river. Yet every room looked too still. Each time she opened a door, the room seemed to startle, like the faces on the masks.

All the rooms were on one side of the hall, just as they had been in the other corridor, only here they were on the right-hand side instead of the left. This detail had struck her as odd when she first saw it, but so many new things were happening that she hadn't had time to wonder about it. Now Roo began to consider this more carefully. The corridor turned gently as she followed it. It seemed to form a large circle, and indeed, after a few minutes she found herself back at her uncle's office.

She remembered her first glimpse of the house from Ms. Valentine's boat. It had looked huge. Yet from the inside it did not seem nearly as big. Maybe it was a trick. Maybe the house was built to impress people with its size when it was really a shell with nothing in the middle. Still, the doorless wall looked newer than the rest of the house, and there were no moldings along the bottom or top. It looked as though the wall were an afterthought, something that was built in a hurry and forgotten. The mystery of the wall nudged at Roo's thoughts, but she could find no good solution to it.

Back in her room she pulled the stolen package from under her shirt and put it on the vanity, then peeled off her wet clothes. She changed into a pair of jeans and a T-shirt from her Hefty bag, then sat by the window and picked at a cheese sandwich that Violet had left for her. She stared out at the rain and the river and the hummocks of grayish green islands. She looked for the island where she had seen the boy on the ice floe, but it wasn't visible from the window. The sky was uniformly gray, with no hint of a break in the storm.

After she finished eating, she examined the stolen envelope. It was addressed to P. Fanshaw and was marked FRAGILE. HANDLE WITH CARE.

Who was P. Fanshaw?

The return address, stamped in dark blue letters, said

it was from Taylor-Baines in Philadelphia. Roo tore open the envelope and looked inside. There was something hard and rectangular, swathed in bubble wrap. She pulled it out, picked off the tape at the seams, and unwrapped it. Inside was a plastic box and in the box was a small bone. It might have come from anything—a dog, a cat. Maybe even the bone of a finger? She shoved it back in the envelope, walked down the hall, and put the envelope in the wooden box under the floorboards in the girls' dormitory.

There, she lay on the chilly floor. The silence in the house had a sound of its own. Thick, pulsing. Waiting. She listened hard for the humming, but it never came.

It was the loneliest afternoon Roo had ever spent.

True, she had never felt the need for other people's company, but she now realized that she had never *ever* been absolutely alone. Even in the trailer's crawlspace, there were living things all around her. Field mice, ants, spiders. There was even a pretty garter snake that would, if she kept very still, slide right onto her sneakers and rest on them. And in the Burrows' woods there were wildflowers and foxes darting past and chipmunks weaving in and out of the underbrush.

But here, in this huge house, life seemed to be hiding from her.

She closed her eyes and thought about the mystery of the walls again. She must have fallen asleep, because the next thing she heard was Violet laughing.

"There you are!" Violet said. She was holding the empty

tray from Roo's lunch and staring down at her with an amused expression on her face. "You're a strange little person. Have you been sitting here all afternoon?"

Roo scrambled to her feet.

"Why are there no doors along one side of all the corridors?" The question sprang from her mind as though she had just been dreaming about it.

"I don't know," Violet answered, looking surprised. "I guess it was just built like that." She turned and started back up the hall, and Roo followed, jogging to keep up with Violet's long-legged stride.

"But there's all this space in the middle of the house, just sitting there," Roo persisted. "Why would someone waste it?"

Violet shrugged. "I guess rich people don't think about things like that. The Summer People around here seem to live by their own rules."

"But my uncle isn't Summer People. He lives here in the winter too," Roo said.

"He didn't always. He only started living here year-round after he was married." Violet blushed, the deep, ruddy blush of a dark-haired girl who has said too much.

"Uncle Emmett is married?" Roo asked, stunned.

After a hesitation, Violet admitted, "Was."

"Are they divorced now?" Roo asked.

"Listen, Roo." She stopped by Roo's bedroom door. "It's not my place to tell you this stuff. Why don't you ask your uncle?"

"How can I ask him anything when he'll barely speak to me?" Roo cried.

Violet's eyes locked onto Roo's. "My mother says that poking around at people's private lives is like rummaging through their bedroom closets. You might find a few interesting knickknacks, but eventually you'll discover something in an old shoebox that you'll wish you hadn't seen."

"I've seen everything," Roo replied evenly.

Violet looked at her with pity—a thing that Roo generally detested but somehow with Violet she didn't mind so much.

"I guess you have." She sighed and then quickly glanced at the stairs, then back at Roo. "Your uncle was married. For a short time. His wife died two years ago."

"How?"

Violet twisted her lips to the left and considered. Outside, the wind must have changed direction because now it rattled the windows as the rain clicked furiously against the glass.

"It was sudden. That's all I know. I didn't work here back then."

"What was her name?" Roo asked, thinking of the package addressed to P. Fanshaw.

"Ana."

That was no good.

"Does anyone else live here?" Roo asked. "Besides my uncle and you and Ms. Valentine?"

Violet cocked her head and blew a puff of exasperation.

"I'm beginning to think they've switched the real Roo Fanshaw for you! Your foster mother told us that you were quiet as a cup, but here you are yammering away with all your questions."

"I have a lot of questions," Roo said, "because everything here is so strange."

"That's just because it's new," Violet said dismissively.

"It *is* strange here!" Roo insisted. "This morning I saw a boy floating down the river on a piece of ice."

Now Violet smiled and shook her head in wonder. "Your first day on Cough Rock and already you've caught a glimpse of the Faigne! People can live here for years and never spot him."

"The Faigne?"

"That's what they call him around here. I think it's an old term from Guernsey. Most of us Donkey Island people have ancestors that come from Guernsey, an island off the coast of England. We still keep a lot of the Guernsey ways and one thing we love is stories of the supernatural. Ghosts, fairies. Sea people."

"I think he made the storm come," Roo said. It popped out of her mouth, and it sounded silly to her own ears as she said it.

"That's not the first time I've heard something like that. There's a fisherman who swears he saw the Faigne flying over Wiggle Room Island on the back of a heron. But then, that particular fisherman is known for sucking down home brew for breakfast. Do you want to know what the Donkey grannies say?"

Roo nodded.

"They say the Faignes are water creatures, not human at all. There's an old story they tell. Many years ago, the water around Guernsey Island had been stormy and violent for months on end. Few local fishermen dared to go out on it, and those who did never came back. So the fishermen got together and thought up a plan. They would send the prettiest girls in the village out on the banks at dusk to try to lure the Faigne to shore, and when he stepped on land, they would capture him and keep him until he promised to quiet the sea. But the Faigne was as cunning as a cat. Every evening he saw one of the girls pacing along the bank. And every evening he just laughed and swam away. One night, though, he saw a girl sitting on a rock in a quiet cove. She was as pretty as the other girls but so odd that the people in the village would have nothing to do with her. Yet she fascinated the Faigne. Night after night they met in this secret cove, talking and laughing, until one day the girl's brother spied on them and told. The next night the fishermen hid, and when the Faigne came on shore to talk to the girl they swooped in and ambushed him. But the Faigne was faster. He and the girl jumped into the water, hand in hand, and the girl was never seen again. But after that, for years and years, whenever someone spotted the Faigne, there was always a lovely snow-white dolphin swimming by his side."

Roo rolled her eyes.

"Yes, well." Violet shrugged. "It's a nice story anyway.

My mother says *our* Faigne is probably just some poor boy without a decent family. I've heard that in the winter he breaks into the homes of the Summer People, and squats there. And in the summer, he camps out on some of the islands. The grannies, heaven love them, fill their hats with food and leave them by the shore when they want the river to stay calm for a ride across to Clayton."

There were quick footsteps on the stairs, and in a moment Ms. Valentine appeared on the landing, looking agitated.

"We need you," she said to Violet in a pinched voice.

Violet glanced quickly at Roo, as if to gauge her reaction, then without a word she hurried downstairs, with Ms. Valentine behind her.

Roo waited a moment. Then she quietly crept downstairs, stopping midway when she had a view of the lobby. Crouching down, she peered through the railing in time to see Violet and Ms. Valentine rushing toward the east wing. Roo padded down the rest of the stairs, then paused to listen. Voices were coming from down the hall in the west wing. The lobby was empty, so Roo scurried across it and headed down the hall, stopping before she came to her uncle's office. Peering around the doorjamb she saw her uncle slumped in an armchair. Dr. Oulette was standing over him, patting the left side of her uncle's face with a cloth.

"It's getting worse," Mr. Fanshaw muttered.

"I told you that it might," Dr. Oulette replied calmly. "Perhaps it's time for a decision—"

"I'll decide when I'm ready," Mr. Fanshaw interrupted.

"Of course you will." Dr. Oulette did not sound at all offended. "Hold still. You're bleeding on your shirt."

"Just let it be, for heaven's sake! I'm fine." Mr. Fanshaw jerked his head away from the cloth, revealing a jagged bite mark on the side of his cheek. "Go tell Ms. Valentine to give you a ride back over to Clayton. We're done for now, I believe."

Roo had been so perplexed at this scene that she heard the footsteps too late. She turned in time to find Ms. Valentine hurrying up the hall, staring at her with fury. Ms. Valentine didn't say a word, which was somehow far more frightening than if she would have bellowed at her. Instead, she opened her eyes wide at Roo, jabbed her finger in the direction of the stairway, and mouthed, "NOW!"

Roo did as she was told. As she sat in bed she tried to make sense of what she had just seen. Who had bitten her uncle like that? It couldn't have been Ms. Valentine or Violet. But then who else was in the house? She thought of the humming. There was someone else living here. Someone who was hidden away.

Roo mulled it over as she waited for Ms. Valentine to come upstairs and reprimand her. But she never did. And that was troubling too.

Chapter 7

The following morning Violet came in carrying a tray of breakfast.

"Good morning," she said brightly when she saw that Roo was awake in her bed.

"Is my uncle okay?" Roo asked, her voice thick from sleep.

"Mr. Fanshaw? He's fine, I guess. Why?"

"He was bleeding last night," Roo said, lifting herself up and resting on her elbows.

"Was he? Maybe he fell," Violet said breezily as she put the tray down on the window seat.

"No. Someone bit his face," Roo said. "I saw it."

"I don't know about that, but I do know this: If I were twelve and the sun was shining"—Violet opened the window, poked her head out for a moment, then pulled it back in and turned to Roo—"I wouldn't be lying in bed, worrying about a little scratch on someone's face."

"It was a bite, not a scratch—," Roo started, but Violet was already heading for the door.

The house was silent and still. Through the open window, Roo heard the lulling sigh of the waves. It was as though the house and everyone in it, even the river itself, were trying to pretend that nothing had happened the night before.

Roo ate, then dressed and hurried downstairs, careful to keep her steps light and quiet. There was no one about, not in the west wing at least. She edged toward the east wing, listening. It was silent here too, though she stopped when she approached the threshold, not quite daring to get caught by Ms. Valentine again.

Outside the air felt as if it had been washed clean. The day was cool but the sun shone. Yesterday's storm had swept the last remaining ice floes from the river. The water was calm now, the crests of its shallow waves turning silver in the sunlight.

Roo picked her way across the path to the bank. When she got there, she gazed at the island with the olive-colored mansion, searching for the boy, the one they called the Faigne. The windows in the house were dark. There was no sign of movement along the terraced landscape. She stared for a long time, waiting for a shifting shadow or a twitching treetop to betray him.

The river began to make a *shush-shush* sound, like a mother comforting her child. It drew Roo's attention away from the house and out toward the water. She watched the ripples rush forward, turning from a fresh blue to a copper color as they came close to shore. She listened to the sound of waves breaking against the banks, as constant and regular as the ticking of a clock. It was so hypnotic that she stood there for some time, listening, until suddenly her eyes darted back to the olive-green house.

She had the funniest feeling that the boy was watching her now. It made her want to duck out of sight, but the rocks by the bank sloped steeply, offering no cover. A few yards off, though, her sharp eyes spotted a rock that jutted out more than the others. It would have been the perfect place to sit and watch the passing boats in summer, but it was the space beneath the rock that interested her. She walked over, glancing surreptitiously toward the olive house, and knelt down beside the rock. There was a tiny crevice between it and the rock below, just large enough for Roo. In a moment, she had squeezed through and found herself in a little cave with enough room for her to sit slightly crouched or to lie down on her side, legs bent.

The view was a good one. She kept her eyes fixed on the olive house, which she could see quite clearly from the cave, sure that if she waited long enough the boy would come out and she could catch another glimpse of him. But when she stayed that way for a good hour and there was still no sign of him, she began to wonder if he really was still there after all.

Sighing, she lay down on her side, her legs bent.

Pressing her ear to the ground, she closed her eyes and listened to the hushed singing in the soil. It was such a tiny, complicated sound that it required the steadiest concentration. The stirring of worms' eggs in their cocoons, the pulse of roots, the minute shifting of bugs. Immediately Roo felt herself relax. Her world collapsed down into a tiny little bundle, just the way she liked it.

After a while another sound rose above the earth's hum. A soft *pid-pad* sound. Roo opened her eyes and looked through the crevice. Something was coming. She kept her body motionless and waited as the sound came nearer, hesitantly, as though nervous. Suddenly a small black-furred face peered into the cave. It was a squirrel, though not the gray type that Roo was used to seeing. This one was charcoal black, with eyes that were bright and quick. He stared curiously at Roo, and she stared back, not daring to move a muscle. They stayed that way for some time until the squirrel suddenly lifted its head. His delicate round ears twitched, and then in a flash he was gone. Roo quickly scrambled out of her hiding place to watch the squirrel dash up the rocks and across the grassy slope, finally disappearing into a tangle of ivy clinging to the house.

A moment later, she heard a boat motor rev up and saw Ms. Valentine pulling out of the lagoon in her Boston Whaler. In the passenger seat was Mr. Fanshaw, and Roo could see a pair of suitcases in the rear of the boat.

He was going away again.

Maybe it was because of what happened last night?

She wondered when he'd be back again. Hadn't Violet said he was often away? It might not be for a very long time. There was no reason for her to care really, but she felt disappointed anyway.

Each morning Roo woke early and wolfed down her breakfast. She had never had much of an appetite back in Limpette, but lately she always seemed to be hungry. After that, she returned to her little cave. She kept a close watch for the Faigne, straining to catch a glimpse of him, but he didn't reappear. Still, she found that the island was full of other surprising things if you paid attention. Polished black water snakes that sunned themselves on the rocks then suddenly leapt into the river to churn the water near the bank. A mossy rock that unexpectedly trundled into the water and swam away, revealing itself to be a snapping turtle. Every day she put her ear to the ground inside the little cave and every day she heard something new. Things were moving more briskly in the earth. The sun was waking things up.

The black squirrel visited with her too. Sometimes he would just peek into the cave, as if to check that she was still there, then scurry away. One time, though, he walked right into the cave and sat with her very companionably, stripping the scales off a pinecone.

"You must be the only squirrel on the island. I haven't seen any others," she said to him.

He looked at her when she spoke, turning the pinecone in his paws. Then he made a chattering noise, which seemed so friendly and encouraging that she spoke to him again.

"I wonder how you got here. I don't think squirrels can swim, so you couldn't leave if you wanted to, could you?"

The squirrel let a pinecone scale drop to the ground and glanced up at her.

"But maybe you like it here."

Later that same day she spied the green mail boat tearing through the river, with Simon LaShomb at the wheel.

I don't mind him, she thought. Then she crawled out of the little cave to watch him approach the lagoon. This time when he held up his hand in greeting, she held hers up too.

"Just the lady I'm looking for!" he called out to her. From the back of his boat, he pulled out four boxes and stacked them up, largest to smallest. "These came for you." He wrapped his arms around the bottom box, gave the stack a quick upward jab with his knee to position it better, then started toward the house. Even with his burden, his long legs glided quickly and easily, so that Roo had to jog to keep up with him

"What's in them?" she asked.

"Too heavy to be tins of herring, too light to be bear cubs. My guess is it's anything in between. Anyway, it's awfully bulky for Ms. Valentine, so I thought I'd just pop round with it. So, Roo Fanshaw, what's the verdict?" He gave her a sidelong glance. "Is Cough Rock growing on you?"

Roo thought for a minute.

"I don't mind it," she said for the second time that day.

Simon laughed. " 'I don't mind it,' she says."

"Why is that funny?" Roo demanded.

"Because you sound exactly like an old River Rat. 'Beautiful day out, isn't it?' 'Oh, I don't mind it.' It's high praise from a River Rat."

"Well, the river has been quiet lately," Roo defended her change of heart. "And no one bothers me here. I can do whatever I want all day long."

"Well, sure, who wouldn't like that?" Simon agreed, though his eyes flitted toward her with some concern, before he started up the front steps.

"Who was that little package for?" Roo asked abruptly. "The one you brought last time."

"Hmm. Mr. Fanshaw, wasn't it? Can you grab the door for me, Roo?"

Roo ran up ahead and pulled open the front door.

"But it was addressed to P. Fanshaw, not E.," Roo said as Simon walked in the house.

"Eh, people are always misspelling names. It's amazing that half the mail ever finds its way to the right place."

He put the boxes down in the lobby and smiled at her. Roo looked at him carefully. His thick, round glasses obscured the expression in his eyes, but she could see nothing in his face to suggest that he was hiding anything.

"Well, whatever's in them"—he slapped the box on top of the stack—"I hope it's something *you don't mind*. So long, Roo."

After he left, Roo sat on the floor, picked up the smallest box and put it on her lap. It was a rectangular package the size of a cutting board. She had never received a package before, much less four of them. The shipping label said:

ROO FANSHAW, COUGH ROCK, CLAYTON, NY 13624

She found it oddly pleasing to see her name attached to the island. Her mind reached out toward the future and cautiously toyed with the idea of a life on Cough Rock. Summers that could be spent outside, all day. The earth would sing loudly and she had all the time in the world to listen to it. And in the winter, she could watch the ice begin to glaze the river, quieting it. It might grow so thick that she could walk out on it. The thought of standing on the river both frightened and excited her. And maybe she would see the Faigne again. Maybe . . . maybe she would even meet him some day. The idea thrilled her though she couldn't quite say why. She had never in her life wanted to know anybody. Maybe it was because he hid too—and he seemed to do it better than she did.

She picked at the edges of the packing tape until it came up and then, slowly, she pulled it off across the box's seam. Lifting the lid she found layers of silver tissue paper with twists of hairline-thin vines printed across it. She lifted up the paper one layer at a time until she uncovered something made of soft, brown material. Pulling it out of the box, the material unfolded, and Roo saw that it was a pair of pants. Brown corduroys, nearly identical to the ones she owned, but new and so velvety that she petted it like a cat. It was her size too.

The second box held sneakers. They weren't the same brand as her own torn-up pair, but the color was nearly the same. The box contained another pair of shoes too, which was nothing like anything she owned but was something she might have chosen for herself—brown and plain with flat rubber soles that would make no noise along the hallways.

The third box held shirts in dark blues and dark greens, the same colors as her own T-shirts, and the last box held several pairs of jeans, some shorts, two nightgowns, and two hooded sweatshirts, nearly exactly like her own.

"What's this?" Violet approached from the east wing, carrying a basket of laundry.

Roo held up one of the sweatshirts.

"Did you order these?" she asked Violet.

"Not me." Violet put down the basket and came over to sift through one of the boxes until she found a packing slip. "Looks like your uncle ordered them."

She picked up a few of the shirts and looked at them quizzically. "The things Ms. Valentine got for you were much nicer."

"I told him I liked my own clothes better," Roo said, remembering.

Violet looked around at the other clothes in the boxes, a surprised expression on her face. "So he bought you your own clothes."

Roo nodded, frowning. Her uncle had barely seemed to notice her; and what he noticed, he hadn't appeared to like.

"I don't know what to think about him," she said, looking up at Violet.

"Yes, well . . . no one really does."

"Do *you* like him?" Roo asked her curiously.

Violet paused, as though she'd never really considered this before. "It's hard to say . . . I doubt he cares if anyone likes him or not. That's why people think he's strange, I guess. It seems unnatural not to care what people think of you, doesn't it? Like a person who never blinks."

"People say that I'm strange," Roo said.

"You are." Violet nestled a sweatshirt back in its box. "But I've seen stranger." She smiled in a private sort of way—a small, sad smile.

Up in her room, Roo tried on all the clothes. They fit perfectly, much better than her old clothes really, which were all stretched out. She peeked in the vanity mirror, standing back so as to see her whole body. Dressed in the new brown corduroys and a green shirt, she looked like a fresher version of herself, as though all the wear and tear of her life had never happened. She raked her hand through her hair. Was it her imagination or did her face look fresher too? The color of her skin and eyes seemed clearer.

"My name is Roo Fanshaw and I live on Cough Rock," she murmured at her reflection. Her voice was timid, but the words themselves sounded right.

"I live on Cough Rock," she repeated with more conviction. "I live with my uncle. He's away a lot. But I don't really mind. I found this little cave—" She stopped, realizing that she was no longer talking to her reflection but imagining what she might say to someone else. The shadowy image of the Faigne popped into her mind.

I might tell him about the cave, she thought. He seems like a person who could keep a secret. I might even tell him about the humming.

"Did you make the storm come?" she whispered to the mirror.

Roo jerked her head up suddenly, and her eyes narrowed. Something had changed in the room. It was such a slight shift that only someone whose senses were as keen as hers would have noticed it. The air quivered. She listened with the same concentration that she listened to the earth. Then she heard it. The humming.

She rushed down the hallway, the humming sound growing more and more distinct until she found herself inside the girls' dormitory. Here, the sound was the loudest, though still muffled. She walked around the room, pressing her ear against the walls, yet she still could not pin down where it came from. It was so distant, yet it was coming from inside the house. Not a ghost. No, this was a person, a living person, she was sure of it. Was it P. Fanshaw? Was it the same person who had bit her uncle's face?

Finally, Roo perched herself on the iron headboard of one of the beds and listened to it. There was nothing frightening in it. In fact, there was something familiar about it, though she couldn't say what. It gave her the same sense of maddening familiarity she had felt when looking at her uncle's face. The same yet not the same. It weaved through the air around her. Sometimes it sounded tentative, as if it were testing something out. Other times it would gain in force, calling out, almost pleading; then, as if it heard itself and was ashamed, it grew soft again.

Suddenly she knew why the humming sounded so familiar. It was exactly how she had sounded back in her own room, all alone and talking to her reflection in the mirror.

Chapter 8

Like most stretches of undisturbed freedom, Roo's came to a sudden and unpleasant end. It happened the following day, while she was sitting in her cave watching a curious bundle of sticks moving across the water in the distance. It had a herky-jerky sort of propulsion that captured her attention. She watched it, squinting, trying to figure out how it could push against the current like that. At the sound of a boat motor starting up, the bundle of sticks swerved abruptly and beneath the sticks a large brown eye gazed in Roo's direction. Roo blew out a breath of surprise and delight. Now she could see the stag's rolling shoulders as it swam past Cough Rock, zigzagging with alarm. The motor sounded like it was coming from the lagoon. Roo poked her head out and craned her neck around the edge of the cave. There was Ms.

Valentine, guiding her Boston Whaler beneath the stone arch and out into the river. That struck Roo as odd. It was too early for her to be collecting the mail. And anyway, she was going in the opposite direction of Choke Cherry Island. Roo watched the boat curl around Cough Rock and disappear from her line of sight.

Abandoning her cave, Roo hurried across the lawn, which the sun had recently coaxed from its dull brown into a bright green. When she reached the semicircular patio she perched on top of the low stone wall that hedged in the patio on one side, and she tracked the Whaler as it plowed across the river toward Clayton.

Maybe my uncle is coming back, she thought.

She felt a rush of nervous anticipation. She wondered if he'd be happy to see that she was dressed in the clothes he'd bought for her—a pair of jeans and a long-sleeved navy blue T-shirt. She looked down at herself. The knees of the jeans had some dirt on them from the cave. She stood up to wipe it off, gave the shirt a tug to smooth it out, then sat back on the wall to watch for Ms. Valentine's return.

The view from the patio looked out onto the seaway, the channel between the islands and Clayton's shores. It was here, Violet had told Roo, that the nurses had once wheeled the hospital's children to sit and watch the ships pass while they breathed the icy air into their weak lungs. Roo wondered if the girl who owned the box under the floorboards had once sat here too, watching the boats zipping past. Speedboats, fancy wooden boats, small aluminum fishing boats. Every so often a massive freighter would lumber between channel markers like a great rust-streaked whale, making the other boats leap up and slam down in its wake.

Finally, Roo spotted the Whaler cutting across the waves and heading back to Cough Rock. As it came closer, Roo could see that there was someone in the passenger seat. Her stomach felt an anxious twist as her eyes strained to make out her uncle's form, but the canopy obscured her view. It was only when the Whaler was finally moored in the lagoon, and the passenger stepped out that Roo saw it was not her uncle at all. It was a woman, thin and gray haired and dressed in a girlish bottle-green jumper dress. From the back of the boat, she hauled out a large, battered suitcase. Ms. Valentine tried to take it from her but the woman waved her away. Ms. Valentine took it anyway, and the two ladies started up the path toward the house.

Roo kept so still that Ms. Valentine might have walked by without noticing her, but the old lady saw her. She stopped in her tracks and said something to Ms. Valentine, whose head then swiveled toward the patio.

"Roo!" Ms. Valentine called. "Come here, please."

Cautiously, Roo hopped off the wall and walked over to them. She didn't like the look of this. Ms. Valentine's expression was worrisomely satisfied, and the gray-haired woman stared at Roo with far too much interest.

"Roo, this is Mrs. Wixton. She's going to be your tutor. *And* your companion."

Mrs. Wixton clasped her hands in front of her dress and nodded to Roo very formally. Her hair was thin and so tightly permed that it looked like she had tiny packing peanuts glued to her scalp.

"I don't want her," Roo said.

"This is what I was talking about," Ms. Valentine said to Mrs. Wixton in a confidential tone.

"I don't need a tutor," Roo insisted.

"The New York State School Board would beg to differ with you, and the local school is not an option," Ms. Valentine retorted. "It's an hour-and-half trip each way. And come winter you won't be able to go in any case, once the river freezes."

"Then let Violet be my tutor," Roo said.

"She has enough to do," Ms. Valentine replied. "And you're the type who needs someone to keep a sharp eye on you."

Roo shot Mrs. Wixton a look of cold resentment. Mrs. Wixton didn't seem to mind. She smiled brightly at Roo. Her lipstick was pale pink—the sort of lipstick that a young girl would wear—but her blue eyes were steady and shrewd.

"Oh, I predict that Roo and I will be best buddies before the week is out," Mrs. Wixton said confidently. She held Roo's angry gaze, undisturbed by Ms. Valentine's impatient shuffling, until Roo finally turned away and looked back out at the river.

Having Mrs. Wixton around was very hard on Roo. No one had ever kept a sharp eye on her before. Mrs. Wixton never left her side. There were hours of lessons every day. Mrs. Wixton had once, many years before, been a middle-school teacher and in her suitcase were stacks of moldy schoolbooks that made Roo sneeze when the pages were turned. At first Roo simply refused to do the lessons, but the old lady was used to dealing with rebellious children. She patiently explained that if Roo continued to disobey her, she'd have to inform Ms. Valentine. "And that would be a pity, since I believe I'm what you would call your 'last hurrah.' If I don't work out, they may not be able to keep you. Ms. Valentine tells me there is a family back where you came from that will take you in . . ."

The threat of being sent back to the Burrows was enough. Roo did Mrs. Wixton's lessons, first furiously, then sullenly. The lessons weren't hard, only long and very dull. At first Roo sped through them quickly, in the hopes of being set free for the rest of the day. But Mrs. Wixton had been told to keep a sharp eye on Roo, and she did her job diligently. Even when Roo was given a break from work and allowed to go outside, Mrs. Wixton accompanied her, always hovering, following along behind her as Roo ran across the rocks. It was unbearable. Roo could not hide in her little cave and watch for the Faigne or listen to the earth. Even the black squirrel would not come out again to see her with Mrs. Wixton there.

The nights were no better. The little room next to Roo's had been hastily furnished and Mrs. Wixton was moved in. There was a narrow bed, a tiny dresser, and that was all. But Mrs. Wixton scrubbed the room and made it tidy and it seemed as if she would be perfectly content to stay there forever.

The first night of Mrs. Wixton's stay, Roo waited until she was sure the old lady was asleep. Then she tiptoed out of her room and started down the hall to listen for the humming. But as she passed Mrs. Wixton's room, Mrs. Wixton called out, "Roo, dear, where are you going?"

And then came the rustle of the old lady easing herself out of bed.

As it turned out, Mrs. Wixton slept as lightly as a cat.

Eventually Roo found a way to break up the monotony of the lessons during the day. She discovered that Mrs. Wixton was fascinated with the Fanshaw family. Every now and then she would interrupt her lesson to casually ask Roo a question about them. "Is this the only house they own?" "Why does your uncle stay all winter?"

At first Roo only shrugged glumly. But soon she realized that Mrs. Wixton would rather hear about the Fanshaws than teach Roo a lesson about geometry. So Roo began to make things up.

She told Mrs. Wixton that her uncle had a fear of birds, and in the spring he would have Ms. Valentine climb all the trees on the property and smash any birds' eggs with a tiny silver hammer, and that one of her cousins had been born without eyebrows, and many other ridiculous things. Mrs. Wixton listened to it all without question. It seemed that there was nothing she wouldn't believe about the Fanshaws, and she never tired of hearing about them.

Sometimes Roo was certain that Mrs. Wixton tailored her lessons to bring up the topic of the Fanshaws. Once when they were studying geography, Mrs. Wixton pointedly said that they would focus on Brazil that day, and she turned her fusty old textbook to a section on the Amazon rain forest. The shiny, yellowed paper held some black-and-white photos of the jungle. Mrs. Wixton flipped through the pages, then stopped at a photo of a squat, thick-bellied man, wearing nothing but a cloth around his waist. In his hand was a limp, lifeless monkey, held by the scruff of its neck.

"Fascinating place, the Amazon," Mrs. Wixton said. "But then you must know quite a bit about it."

"Why would I?" Roo asked irritably.

"Because of *her*," Mrs. Wixton said. "Your aunt. Mr. Fanshaw's late wife." She was baiting Roo, trying yet again to glean some information about Uncle Emmett. But this time, Roo herself was interested.

"I never met her," Roo said.

"But you must have heard about her," Mrs. Wixton pressed.

Roo shook her head, hating to admit it, yet hoping that Mrs. Wixton would tell her more.

"Well, she came from Brazil, apparently. A little village on the edge of the rain forest. Her name was Ana. Your uncle spotted her on one of his trips and was instantly smitten, or so the story goes." Mrs. Wixton was clearly thrilled to be able to offer up information that Roo didn't have. "I saw her once in Clayton with Mr. Fanshaw. She was quite striking, with beautiful long black hair. But she had a wild look about her. I felt sorry for her, I actually did. Fish out of water. Though of course your uncle was so kind to her," she added carefully. "All that gossip after she passed away made me sick to my stomach."

"What gossip?" Roo asked.

"Oh, folks around here will say anything, especially if it's about Summer People."

"What did they say?"

"Well," Mrs. Wixton began, rising off the bed for a moment to adjust her skirt, "some people believe she was murdered." She waited a beat to see that she had Roo's full interest before she continued. "It was because her death was so strangely sudden. She had been perfectly healthy and well, according to the people who had been working in this house. And then, quite out of the blue, she was dead. And to make matters worse, your uncle refused to speak about it. He immediately fired everyone who had been in the house, except Ms. Valentine. It made people suspicious."

"Who do they think killed her?" Roo asked.

Mrs. Wixton now shifted on the bed, straightening her spine and crossing her legs. "Of course it was all malicious nonsense."

"They don't think it was my uncle, do they?" Roo asked, shocked. Her uncle had seemed cold and hard, but killing his own wife . . . she couldn't imagine it.

"How did we get on this topic in the first place?" Mrs. Wixton looked at Roo as if it had been her idea. "Okay, hocus-pocus, let's try to focus." She patted the pages of the textbook.

As the days wore on, Roo's captivity became harder and harder for her to bear. The bright spring light teased at her through the windows. She ached to be outside. The sun was melting deeper into the ground, waking everything up. The earth would be singing by now, and she was missing it! A hundred times a day she felt ready to bolt out of the room, fly down the stairs, and run outside to freedom. But the threat of being sent back to the Burrows kept her rooted. Gradually she began to feel sleepy and slow witted. Her pencil would droop in her hand while her mind wandered, though when Mrs. Wixton jolted her with a small shake and asked her what she was daydreaming about, she couldn't remember.

She was glad for any time outdoors, even if she was under constant guard by Mrs. Wixton. As soon as she felt the sun on her skin she awoke. She ran around the island, knowing that Mrs. Wixton could not keep up; yet also knowing that there was nowhere really for her to go. She was desperate for freedom and for solitude, even if it was only for the few minutes when she was on one side of the island and Mrs. Wixton was on the other. It was during one of these runs when Roo had sprinted to one end of the island, leaving Mrs. Wixton far behind, that she saw the familiar jutting rock, which hid the little cave. In a flash she ducked inside.

Chapter 9

She kept still and quiet, which was the easiest thing in the world for her to do. She watched Mrs. Wixton pass once, then twice more. On the third pass, Mrs. Wixton was calling for her, though not very loudly.

She doesn't want them to know that she's lost me, Roo realized.

By her fifth pass Mrs. Wixton's voice was sounding panicked. Her skinny legs moved faster. Roo couldn't help but smile. The calls were louder and lasted for some time. Then they went quiet.

Roo wondered what would happen next. But when nothing did, she knew that nothing would. Mrs. Wixton wouldn't want Ms. Valentine to know that her famously sharp eye was not quite sharp enough. She wouldn't tell her that Roo was missing, not for as long as possible, and that would give Roo a few hours of beautiful freedom.

She curled up and lay down on her side, ear to the earth, and listened to the music. It was busy and insistent now, pulsing with energy. She slipped into the sound gratefully, the way a numb, cold body slips beneath warm blankets. When she had her fill, she propped herself up on one elbow and pushed her finger into the dirt, scraping until she found a thick pink-and-gray earthworm. She held it, watching as it nudged its tapered head in the palm of her hand to stop itself and let the rest of its body contract in ripples. After a while, Roo placed it back on the ground, poking her finger in the earth to give it a tunnel. It was then that she spied something on one side of the hole. A piece of green-and-white-striped paper. Carefully she extracted it. It was a Juicy Fruit gum wrapper with a red wax-paper wrapper inside. The same wrapper as the gum in the box beneath the floorboards. Roo remembered the flashlight in the box. Maybe the girl had found this cave too, all those years and years ago, and had escaped here, just like she had. Roo wondered if the girl had gotten well and gone home. But then she looked down at the ring with the two hearts, still on her finger. No, the girl had probably died here. She would have taken the ring with her if she had lived.

Roo stayed in her little cave for hours, watching the river change colors. Each time she thought she would finally come out of hiding, the river kept her rooted, enchanting her as its waves shifted from silver to copper to indigo. Evening approached, and she watched the sun slide down in the sky until it was just a splinter above the dark water. Layers of coral and pink smudged the horizon, peppered by a flock of Canada geese, their gulping barks bouncing off the surface of the river.

It began to grow chilly. Roo stretched her sweatshirt over her knees and huddled for warmth as she stared out at the water, black and silver now and moving gently, like a mind before sleep.

The water hissed suddenly. She remembered how it had reminded her of a snake when she first saw it. It hissed again, louder this time, and Roo lifted her head off her knee, frowning out at the river. There was a shadow moving along the southern edge of the island. It was long and narrow and it glided smoothly, like an alligator.

For the first time that day, Roo poked her head out of the cave. She glanced around quickly, making certain that no one was nearby. Then she crawled out of the cave and stood, stretching her cramped limbs. A cloud had drifted over the crescent moon, making the night so black that Roo had to search the river for some time before she spotted the shadow again. It had glided surprisingly far along the perimeter of the island. It drifted closer and closer to her before finally stopping several yards away. There it stayed, near to the banks, bobbing on the waves. Slowly, Roo approached the thing, making small decisions about it as she went along: It has a round head, a long snout. A bird? Too large for a bird. There, it moved! Some sort of animal?

When she finally reached it she saw that it was not an animal at all. It was a canoe, and sitting inside it was a boy of about fourteen with very pale hair tied back in a short ponytail. By the time she realized who she was looking at, she found that he was staring right back at her.

"You're that boy," Roo said, remembering to keep her voice low despite her surprise. "The Faigne."

The boy smiled at her, as though he were pleased she had heard of him. "You can call me Jack."

"What are you doing here?" she asked.

"The river took me," he said. "She was curious about you."

"That's not true. You paddled over here, I saw you."

"I was curious too," he said simply.

The moon sailed out from behind the clouds. Now she could see the boy more clearly. In the past, Roo had never thought much about boys. They had only ever teased her or called her trailer trash. Certainly she had never thought about the way they looked. But this boy, Jack, was so beautiful that it was alarming. She stared at him, as though his beauty were some sort of trick. He stared back in such a frank, pleased way that it embarrassed her.

"Do you really live on the river?" she asked him, trying to regain her composure.

"That's right." He watched her with an easy smile. He seemed to be asking his own questions about Roo without speaking a word, and finding the answers in her face.

"Where's your family?" she asked.

He gestured vaguely toward the far shores.

"Why don't you live with them?" Roo asked.

He hesitated, then replied lightly, "I prefer the river."

But Roo knew better. She knew that unless things were very bad at home, you still would rather be with your family.

Suddenly a black shadow swooped down from the sky. It was a heron, the tip of its tremendous wing skimming the air just above Jack's head. It gave off a single harsh croak then flew away again.

"Someone's coming," Jack said, and with a push of his paddle, his canoe slid away.

Roo ran back into the little cave, squeezed in, and peered out of the opening in time to see Jack's canoe melt into the black sky and disappear. The wind began to settle. The river seemed to stretch itself out, smoothing out its ripples, and the air grew less chilled. In a moment a pair of legs passed the cave opening. Mrs. Wixton. Roo heard her footsteps stop a few yards away, then they retraced their path past the cave. Soon the house door thumped closed and all was quiet again.

She should go in, she knew she should. But instead she watched the black water late into the night, listening carefully for the hiss of a canoe paddle and the slow flapping of a heron's wings.

She hadn't meant to fall asleep, and when she awoke, it was to the sound of a violent downpour. She had no idea what time it was. From the lifting darkness outside, she guessed it was early morning. Five or six o'clock maybe. She poked her head through the cave's opening to blink out at the rain. It bullied the island with its hard pecks, while thunder roared across the water and lightning flashed in the sky.

Roo glanced up at the house. The lights on the first floor were off. There were no lights on in the east wing and one light in the west wing. Mrs. Wixton was probably in a state of panic by now. Good.

Roo crawled through the opening and made a run for it across the rocks and over the muddy lawn to the front door. Once in her bedroom she sat on her bed and steeled herself for Mrs. Wixton. The old lady would certainly be listening for her in the next room. But when minutes passed and she didn't appear, Roo stole into the hallway and peered into Mrs. Wixton's bedroom. It was empty, the blankets on the bed neatly arranged.

The rain was pounding against the windows, but underneath the sound Roo now could hear another one coming from down the hall—the sound of someone crying.

Stupid woman! Roo thought. *Ms. Valentine will hear her!*

Roo hurried down the hallway, her anger growing by the second.

"Stop it! Stop it, Mrs. Wixton!" she called out as loud as she dared to. "I'm right here!"

She followed the awful bawling into the children's dormitory. Here it was loudest but when she looked around, she found that the room was empty. There was a sudden, distant drumming sound—a fist against a wall maybe—and the crying changed to shrieks, raw and anguished. It was not Mrs. Wixton who was crying. The voice was too high, too young.

Every so often, people do things that are difficult to explain. Out of the blue, a person might suddenly feel like she should pull back a loose wallboard in her barn only to discover an abandoned litter of kittens hidden there. That morning, as the watery orange sun began to rise, Roo noticed a tiny, guttering light enter the children's dormitory and dance across the floor. It climbed the far wall, like a spider lit from inside, until it finally settled on the brass latch of a little cabinet door set in the wall. Roo walked up to it, reached out to touch the light, and it was gone. All that was left was her hand on the cabinet latch and the oddest feeling that she should open it.

Chapter 10

Roo unhooked the latch and gave the cabinet door a yank. She thought it felt too heavy for such a small door until she realized that it was actually much larger than it looked. In fact, it was not a cabinet at all, but a door that stretched all the way down to the floor, its edges cleverly concealed in the beadboard wainscoting. As the door opened, cold damp air rushed out, smelling of stone and mold. Inside was a tunnel, neatly hewn out of granite. The ceiling was low but the tunnel was wide, and so long and dark that Roo could not see the end of it.

Roo stepped in, careful to let the door stay slightly ajar. There were gas lamps fastened to the wall, their glass globes shrouded in dust. Whatever this was, it looked as if no one had been there for a very long time. The crying was louder here. The farther Roo walked down the tunnel, the louder the crying became, until it seemed to pulse out of the stone walls. Roo could make out rhythms in the way the voice rose and fell, as if it were saying something, though she could not hear any real words. Finally the crying grew so loud that Roo squinted through the darkness, almost expecting to see the filmy shape of the Yellow Girl emerge in front of her.

Instead, she saw a door. It signaled the end of the tunnel. The pitch of the crying rose, like a question, then stopped. The crying had come from the other side of the door, Roo was sure of it. Reaching out, her hand closed over the knob and she turned it a little, making it squeal softly. She winced then paused to listen. There was only silence, but she sensed the person on the other side of the door was listening for her too.

Taking a deep breath, she gripped the knob and tried to turn it more. It wouldn't move. She pushed against the door, but it wouldn't budge either. It must have been locked from the other side.

"Is someone in there?" Roo whispered. She waited, but there was no answer. Stepping back, she looked around to see if there was another way in. There were no other doors, just solid stone walls all around.

Still, something caught her eye. It was on the wall near the floor, a disc of smooth blackness. Roo walked up to it, then crouched down to get a better look. It was an opening in the wall, perfectly round and so cool to the touch that it must have been lined with metal, though it was too dark to see.

Roo dropped down on all fours and ducked her head inside. She couldn't see much, so she shimmied her body into the opening, crawling cautiously across the slick, cold metal. A second later she realized her mistake. The metal floor suddenly gave way beneath her, inclining so sharply that she found herself shooting headlong down the slippery tube. It was so surprising that she slid down several yards before she thought to brace herself against the sides, stopping her descent. But this was no good either, since she couldn't turn around in the tight space and it was too steep to climb back up to the top. She had no choice but to keep going down.

Stretching her fingers out ahead of her, she pressed them against the metal, which enabled her to awkwardly crawl downward. The tube went on and on. She could not see the end of it. Her arms soon grew tired from holding herself back, so she relaxed her hands and let herself slide. She quickly picked up speed and just when she thought she'd better stop herself again, the tunnel angled up slightly, slowing her down.

In a moment, the tunnel walls opened out and she came to a halt on top of a flat metal platform. Cautiously, she rose and looked around. She was in a dark room with a low ceiling canopied with pipes. Wires hung down from some of the walls and there were large metal tanks in the corners.

She was in the basement.

It was then that Roo realized she had just traveled down the "body chute," the tunnel that the old sanitarium had used to hide its human losses. The thought that she had slid down the same chute as so many dead children, bundled in yellow sheets, made the nape of her neck feel icy.

It was a long, long time ago, Roo told herself. *Years and years.*

Still, she hurried off the platform and gazed around the dark room, letting her eyes adjust so she could find a way out.

There. Along one of the walls, she could make out the shape of a door. She started toward it, but something ratlike passed close to her feet and made her jump. She never minded snakes or spiders or mice or other things that people were normally afraid of, but rats made her feel queasy. She stared around at the floor, trying to spot it so that it wouldn't surprise her again. A movement from beside an overturned pail caught her eye, and a black shadow leapt forward. Roo sucked back her breath. But then she recognized the black squirrel. He approached slowly, stopping and starting, as if giving her time to remember who he was.

Roo knelt down and smiled. "Is this where you live? In this nasty basement?"

The squirrel stood up on its haunches, its bright eyes trained on her for a few seconds. Then it dropped down to all fours and scurried away behind a metal panel that stood, floor to ceiling, at one end of the room. The panel had many switches and timers, but there were wires dangling from the back of it that looked as if they had been cut.

Roo waited for the squirrel to return, and when he didn't she followed him to see where he had gone. The panel, she discovered, had a flight of wooden stairs behind it, and the squirrel was sitting patiently on the third step, waiting. At the sight of her, he darted up the rest of the stairs and slipped through a small hole in the ceiling.

Roo frowned up at the hole, noting that it was, in fact, a gnawed-out bit of a trapdoor, lying flush with the ceiling. Climbing to the top of the steps, Roo put her hand flat on the little door and gave it a small push, expecting it to be locked. To her surprise, the door flipped over on its hinges, and a *whoosh* of warm, moist air hit her face. The smell was musty and earthy. High above her, she could see the pale early morning sky, making her think that she had found an entrance to the outside. But in a moment, she realized that she was seeing the sky through hundreds of tiny panes of glass shaped in diamonds and forming a clear dome that stretched up as high as the house itself.

Climbing the last step, she hoisted herself out of the basement and gazed around in astonishment. The glass dome enclosed what looked like an ancient, brittle jungle. Dead trees towered up out of the dirt floor. Their branches were thin, many broken and hanging, trapped within the spindly arms of other branches. Thick, ropy vines twisted around the dead trees, climbing up to the very top then tumbling down in thick gray sheets, like grim waterfalls. Clinging to some of the panes on the dome were brown creepers, pressing themselves against the glass as though pleading to be let out. Underfoot, there were spiny bushes and collapsed ferns and limp brown plants, and everything, all of it, was dead.

It was the saddest and most beautiful place Roo had ever seen.

"What happened here?" she whispered.

There was only silence, yet she could *feel* an answer trying to push out, mute but struggling to be heard. Stepping in farther, she saw a patch of slate gray beneath the undergrowth and found a flagstone footpath. She followed it, nudging away the dead plants that covered it most thickly as she went. The path twisted through the atrium, following the contours of a gentle incline until it ended below a shelf of rock that formed a small cliff. There were smaller rocks alongside the little cliff, and these Roo used as footholds to climb, with some difficulty, to the top of the rock shelf. Beside it stood a large boulder. Roo sat on it and looked down at the ruined garden, at the towering gray trees and the wraithlike tangle of drooping branches.

If there were ghosts in this house, she thought, *this is where they would live.*

A scratching sound from above startled her. She looked up in time to see a branch on one of the great trees shiver. She did not believe in ghosts, but still she held her breath as she stared at the tree. Its trunk was completely encased by a thick vine that coiled around it, right to the tip of the uppermost branch. And there, on the narrow end of the branch, was the black squirrel. Roo watched as he leapt to another branch and raced across it.

"How can you stand it, being the only living thing in this place?"

It was then that she noticed a patch of leaves on the ground, near one of the atrium walls, which were much darker than the rest—almost black. Sliding off the boulder, she walked to the dark spot and kneeled down to inspect it. To her surprise she found that the leaves were damp. Everything else in the garden was bone dry, yet here . . . She leaned forward and poked a finger deep into the leaves. The soil was wet too. She gazed around, looking for the water source, finally finding it when she glanced up. There was a broken pane on the dome, close to the edge. The morning light was growing brighter now, and the rain had stopped, but Roo could just make out the path of rivulets, trailing down the wall of the atrium and ending near the patch of damp leaves. She raked the thick layer of leaves to one side and yanked up the dead grass beneath it, exposing a patch of bare soil. With the sun beating down on the damp spot, maybe something could grow there.

She squinted up at the ceiling, searching for other broken panes, and found several more. It was all the encouragement she needed. Roo went to work, tugging at the dead grass and plants around the damp spots, gathering up the dried leaves and piling them in a corner. The black squirrel inched up to her once, to see what she was doing. He came so close that she could have reached out and stroked his fur, but Roo was so busy working that she hardly noticed him.

She worked for hours until she was drenched with sweat, and so thirsty that her throat stung. Finally, she sat back on her heels, exhausted but happy. The sun was pouring into the atrium now, bathing the garden in pale light. The little plots of bare dark earth looked so promising that she leaned down, put her ear to the ground, and listened.

Astonishingly, she heard nothing at all.

That had never happened before. Even in the crawl space under the trailer, in the middle of winter, she could hear life beneath the soil; it was a languid, subtle sound, but it was there.

In this garden, though, there was only silence. It was the nothingness of death. Frighteningly permanent. The garden had been erased from the world, in the same way that her father had been erased, extinguishing everything that he was—the good and the bad.

Once more she pressed her ear to the earth. Concentrating fiercely, her sensitive ears strained to hear a sound, the smallest sound. She stayed that way for a long time, motionless, eyes closed. Then, after many minutes, she thought she heard something. It was weak and frayed around the edges, and it came and went, like shallow, feverish breathing. Sometimes it fell silent for so long, Roo thought it had stopped altogether. But after a while it would start again, struggling. So fragile, so almost-not-there.

"Stay alive," Roo pleaded.

Chapter 11

It was late morning when Roo finally left the garden. The door that led outside was badly warped and stuck tight, but with some effort she managed to budge it. A thick covering of ivy pulled away from the house as the door opened. Now she could see why she had never noticed the door before; the vines had grown so thickly over this side of the house that it had completely concealed it. This was the back of the house, too, where the space between the banks and the house itself was so narrow, and the drop so precipitous, that Roo hadn't spent much time there.

Outside, the sun shone bright but the air felt cool against her hot, damp skin. As she started back toward the front entrance of the house, she plotted how she might return to the garden. It would be tricky to get past

Mrs. Wixton again. Maybe she could make some sort of deal with the old lady. She wouldn't run off again if Mrs. Wixton would give her an hour a day to herself. She could do a lot in an hour. She could clear the garden more thoroughly, getting rid of all the dead branches and leaves. The garden would need water too—the little trickles from rainwater weren't enough. She could haul in water from the river.

Roo had just rounded the corner of the house, when a voice came from down by the banks.

"Was this your little hidey-hole?"

Turning sharply, Roo saw Violet kneeling by the jutting rock that marked the little cave. "You must be part snake to have squeezed in there," Violet said.

"Mrs. Wixton told," Roo said.

"Mrs. Wixton has been fired."

"Really?" Roo's voice brightened at the news, but Violet's expression was uncharacteristically grim.

"We found her looking around some empty rooms this morning. Ms. Valentine got suspicious." Violet shook her head, her brown eyes severe. "Do you realize we've been turning the house inside out all morning, looking for you? Ms. Valentine's been frantic. She thought you might have drowned."

"And now she'll see that I'm fine," Roo replied.

She met Violet's gaze, but Violet looked away.

"What?" Roo asked. Her stomach suddenly felt queasy. "What will she do?" She watched Violet's mouth tighten. "Will she send me away?"

"This is not a good place for you, Roo."

"Yes, it is," Roo insisted, her voice rising.

"No, Roo. It's not really a good place for anyone."

"*You* stay," Roo accused.

"I'm paid to stay. I have three little sisters back on Donkey and a mom who's raising them on her own. I need this job. And I'm needed here. You're not."

Roo thought of the garden, of the freshly cleared earth, bare now but full of possibilities.

I am *needed here,* she thought.

"Come on," Violet said. She walked over to Roo and took her hand, squeezing it once. "Let's go inside and get this over with. Ms. Valentine will be so relieved to see you she might forget to tear you into bits and feed you to the gulls."

Ms. Valentine *was* relieved. In fact, at the sight of Roo, she rushed up and hugged her; but the hug was brief and the fury quickly followed.

"We've tried with you, Roo, we've tried, even Mr. Fanshaw cannot deny we've tried but now I'm done. What were you thinking? Do you realize what a panic you put us into? We thought you were dead. No, no, this won't work. We should have never taken you here in the first place."

Roo opened her mouth to protest, but Ms. Valentine held up her hand. "Mr. Fanshaw gave me leave to make this decision. I hate to do it but you've forced my hand. I've made arrangements for the Burrows to take you back."

"No!" Roo cried.

"You'll be able to go to your own school, in your own town. It's where you belong—"

"I belong here!" Roo insisted, and then she surprised everyone, including herself, by bursting into tears. For a moment, Ms. Valentine and Violet just stared at her, not knowing what to do.

"The Burrows are good people, Roo . . . ," Ms. Valentine said, her voice softening. But Roo was not crying about the Burrows, as much as she hated the thought of living with them and all the other foster children again. She was not even crying because she would have to leave Cough Rock, which she had grown to love. Her tears were for the garden. She felt it tug at her like nothing ever had before. If she left, no one would care about it. No one would try to help it. It would remain a graveyard. Not quite dead and not quite alive, which seemed to Roo to be worse than death.

Violet wrapped her arm around Roo's shoulder and led her upstairs. She didn't try to console Roo—Violet saw that it would do no good. Instead she removed Roo's muddy shoes and put her straight into bed. She pulled the blankets up to Roo's chin, kissed her softly on her forehead, as though she were sick, and let her be.

For a long while Roo lay very still, staring up at the ceiling, while her body went through the small hiccupping aftershocks of a hard cry. She tried to tuck her thoughts in, as she always did, making them very small. But for the first time in her life, it wouldn't work. She could feel her thoughts flexing against their confinement, the way a foot pushes against a shoe that it's outgrown. She could not keep her mind from the garden. She imagined the sun beating down on the soil now that the weeds and leaves were cleared. What if it didn't rain for a while? The areas she had cleared would become as dry as dust. Had she made things worse by trying to help? Her worries went around in circles. Eventually the small hiccups began to subside, and her breathing grew quiet. That was when she heard the crying again. It stopped her thoughts, made her sit up, and listen harder. The crying was steady, emotionless but imploring, like a bird calling out to another bird.

Throwing off her covers, Roo jumped out of bed. She felt a sudden, angry determination to find the source, once and for all. She hurried to the girls' dormitory and went straight to the secret door in the beadboard cabinet. This time she entered the passageway with more confidence. She headed straight for the door at the end of the passage, but at the sight of the black round chute to the garden she hesitated. She could go down there now. She could haul water in from the river and pour it on the soil. It wouldn't be enough, but it might help a little.

The crying grew more insistent, as if the person knew she was there. Forcing her attention back to the door, Roo put her hand on the knob and turned it, expecting it to be locked again. But this time the knob turned all the way. The crying suddenly stopped. Whoever was on the other side must have been watching the door, waiting for her.

It made her stomach feel tight and she wavered, thinking about the bite mark on her uncle's face. Pressing her ear to the door, she listened. She didn't hear anything, but once again she sensed someone listening for her as well.

I'm fast, she reassured herself. *I'm fast and small. If I have to, I can outrun whoever this is.*

She took a breath, turned the knob, then inched the door open, so that if something started to come out, she could slam the door fast.

On the other side of the door was a chair. And sitting in the chair was a boy. He stared at her with a look of both terror and anticipation, his dark, deeply shadowed eyes still damp from crying. In an instant, though, his expression changed to irritation.

"Who are you?" he demanded.

He looked to be a little younger than Roo, and was as skinny as she was; but while Roo was hard and wiry, he looked withered. His blue pajamas drooped on his thin frame.

"Stop staring at me!" he screamed at her.

"Are you the one who's always humming?" Roo asked.

"Who *are* you? I don't know you."

"I live here," Roo said, though that would change very soon.

"No, you don't. There's only me and my father here."

"Who's your father?"

"Emmett Fanshaw, who do you think? There's only me and him. And the help. Oh"—he sat up straighter and looked at her very imperiously—"did they hire you to clean? I hope so. Violet is too clumsy. She's broken five of my bones since she's started here."

"That's a lie," Roo said. "And I'm not your maid, I'm your cousin."

She started to close the door then, but the boy called out, "Wait!"

Roo stopped, glaring back at him.

"What?"

"You can't be my cousin," the boy said, his voice less disdainful now. "I don't have any cousins."

"I'm your cousin because our fathers were brothers."

The boy thought about this. "I remember once hearing something about my father's brother." He looked up at Roo, and she braced herself for him to say something awful about her father. Instead, the boy stood and said, "All right then. You can come in and see my coyote."

Roo drew back her head, one eyebrow raised dubiously. "You have a coyote in your room?"

"A small one."

Chapter 12

Roo hesitated. She didn't like the boy, and she doubted very much that he had a coyote in his room. In the end, though, she gave in to her curiosity.

The room was very large and the drawn curtains made it dark, but Roo could see that it had the same long rectangular shape as the girls' dormitory.

This must have been where the boys slept, Roo thought. *And they also had a door that led to the body chute.*

This room was far more luxurious, though. The furniture was formal and heavy, with a large four-poster bed in one corner. There was a stone fireplace whose mantel held stacks of board games and books. The other end of the room was lined with shelves, and on the shelves were dozens of animal skeletons mounted on wooden blocks.

"I'm still working on the coyote," the boy said, pointing to a large skeleton that sat on a desk in the corner. It was propped up with metal posts and wire, and there were bottles of glue and a small drill on the desk. The coyote was such a spindly thing, it seemed to be made up of birch branches bent to form a spine and legs and the most delicate toes imaginable. The skeleton tilted to one side, as though it were limping, and Roo noticed that the bottom part of its right hind leg was missing.

"Are they real bones?" Roo asked, reaching toward one of the coyote's legs.

"Don't touch. Yes, of course they're real."

The boy watched Roo as she walked around the room, examining the shelves. There were birds, frogs, lizards, coiled snakes. She stopped at a skeleton with a long tail that was shaped like a conical seashell and what looked to be half a beehive covering its back.

"Armadillo," the boy said. "Look at the joints in the shell. That's how they can roll up in a ball. And that one there . . ." He pointed to a long, squat skeleton with impossibly fine ribs and the head of a tiny dinosaur. "A Gila monster. She was tricky to put together. The coyote was easy." He ran his finger lightly over the coyote's front leg. "See how the elbows turn in and the feet turn out. That's so the legs can swing in a straight line. Makes them faster. But Violet snapped one of the metatarsals on this hind leg, so I'm waiting on a new one. What do you think?"

"I think it's creepy," Roo said.

"That's what Violet says. But it's not very different from doing a puzzle. When things are all in pieces, don't you want to put them together again? I do."

He seemed more likable somehow now, Roo thought. More like a regular boy. She looked at him carefully, taking in his bony shoulders, slightly curled in like an old man's, and the bruised purple shadows beneath his eyes. His wide jawline made it seem as if he were meant to be more substantial than he was. His lips were full, though dry and pale, and his hair was black and thick and wild looking.

"What's your name?" Roo asked.

"Phillip. What's yours?"

"Roo. How come I've never seen you around the house before? Or out by the water?"

The question appeared to displease him.

"I prefer my room." His tone grew cold and self-important again. It reminded Roo of his father. "I suppose you don't know how to play canasta?"

"No."

"You'll learn." He walked over to the fireplace and took two packs of cards from the top of the mantel. Then he sat down on his bed and stared at Roo, his back stiff and head held high, waiting.

"Well?" he said when Roo didn't move.

"I never said I would play," Roo replied.

"But I *want* you to play," Phillip said, looking genuinely shocked, as if no one had ever denied him a thing in his entire life.

"Then you had better *ask* me to—nicely—not order me around like I'm your servant."

Phillip opened his mouth to say something—and from the look on his face it wasn't going to be anything polite. But then he shut his mouth again. After staring up at the ceiling for a moment, he looked back at Roo.

"Please," he said stiffly.

It was just short of civil, but Roo accepted it.

The game was complicated and Roo had to focus. But she was a fast learner and before long her thoughts began to wander back to the garden.

"I'd better go," she said finally, laying down her cards.

"But why?" Phillip cried.

"I have things to do."

"What things? *What things?*" he demanded, his voice growing sharp.

"It's none of your business what I do," Roo retorted.

"It is my business! It's *my* house!" Then his anger turned to shrieks: *"Don't go, don't go, don't go!"* until a door on the far side of the room was flung open and in rushed Ms. Valentine and Violet. At the sight of Roo, Ms. Valentine's mouth popped open. She looked from Phillip to Roo and back again, as if unable to convince herself that she was seeing them both together.

"How did this happen?" she asked in a thin, horrified voice.

Violet hurried past her and gripped Roo by the shoulder, quickly guiding her out the door and shutting it. She turned to Roo, poised to scold.

"Don't!" Roo warned her. "It doesn't matter anyway. You couldn't drag me back in there. I don't know how you can stand him, I really don't. He's awful."

"Not awful, Roo," Violet said. "He's just had a rough time of it."

"So have a lot of other people."

"Like you?" Violet asked.

"Well, you don't hear me screeching, do you?" Roo said.

Phillip's screams filled the hallway, interspersed with Ms. Valentine's attempts to calm him down.

"No, I don't," Violet agreed. "You suck it all in. You keep yourself as hard as a steel beam. Phillip lets it rip, but in a few minutes he'll be done. He'll go limp and I can hug him and wipe his eyes and cheer him up. Which is better? I don't know."

"Anyway," said Roo, shaking this off, "why did you keep us a secret from each other? You lied to me when I asked about the humming."

Violet sighed, blinked quickly, and glanced away. After a moment she said, "Phillip is strung tight as a fiddle. There's no denying he's lived a strange life, cooped up on this island with no other children around and his father gone so much. He adored his mother and she adored him back. She was all he had, really, and they were always together, best friends. So when she died—well, it shattered the poor thing." Violet shook her head. "I've never seen a person grieve so hard. He just stays in his room all day, tinkering with those awful bones, growing more gloomy and sullen. He barely eats a thing. He's just wasting away. We thought it might help him if he had friends, so this past summer Ms. Valentine arranged for some children to visit him. Two brothers close to Phillip's own age who live on Murray Island. They came once, but while they were here Phillip went into a rage, screaming and breaking things."

"He was the one who bit my uncle's face?" Roo guessed.

Violet nodded. "Mr. Fanshaw is worried—we're all worried—about his mental state. He's convinced himself of all kinds of odd things. It just seemed best to keep the two of you apart for a while. We were going to tell him about you eventually, of course. We wanted him to get used to the idea before he met you." She paused, a little smile starting on her lips. "My mother thought that was foolish. She thought we should let you and Phillip meet. She said two strong tempers are like a pair of waves coming at each other. Sometimes they smooth each other out."

"Well, obviously that didn't work," Roo said, jabbing a thumb back at Phillip's door. The shrieking had now changed over to wild sobs.

"What did you say to him anyway?"

"Nothing!" Roo insisted. "All I did was start to leave. He wanted me to stay."

Violet laughed. "Well, maybe Mom was right after all. When I first met you, I thought you and your cousin were much of a muchness."

When Roo screwed up her face, Violet explained, "It

means you two are just the same. Both of you so proud and snappish." She rubbed her knuckles gently against Roo's chin. "What do you think? Can you stay out of trouble for the rest of the day?"

Roo wasted no time. As soon as Violet went back upstairs to Phillip, Roo went outside and walked the perimeter of the house until she came to the overgrown ivy that concealed the basement door. She glanced around quickly before she opened it a crack and slipped through.

Once inside the garden, Roo went to work straightaway, clearing more dead grass and leaves, adding to the pile in the corner. She strained and pulled at roots till her hands were red and her shoulders ached.

In the basement she found an old bucket caked with dried cement and took it outside to the river. There were many boats on the water today. The Summer People had begun to arrive. Only a few weeks ago, Roo would have admired the fearless way they plowed through the waves in their speedboats and Jet Skis, but now they seemed only careless and clumsy. She thought of Jack's silent approach in his canoe; the way he rode the river as easily as a loon. Glancing over at the island with the olive-green house, she saw that there was now a boat docked by the pier. Four candy-colored Adirondack chairs were set outside the front of the house. Jack would be long gone. She wouldn't get to see him again before she left. It bothered her to think about that. Would he wonder what had happened to her?

Pretty soon she'd be back at the Burrows' house. She thought about the cramped room she would have to share with the other foster girls. When they saw her, they would know that she had been tossed out of her uncle's house. They would love that. Roo felt her face heat up and her muscles tighten. The tinny voice of an approaching tour boat spliced into her thoughts.

"—at a time when it was thought fresh, cold air could help in the treatment of tuberculosis. Unfortunately, the sanitarium killed more children than it healed. It finally closed its doors in 1961 and the island is now privately owned."

Roo quickly dragged the side of the bucket on the bottom of the shallows, scooping up as much water as she could hold, then hauled the bucket back into the garden before the tour boat swung around the island into view.

Back in the garden, she tipped the bucket and let the water spill out onto the soil, walking backward. By the time the bucket was empty, only a narrow swath of earth had been dampened. It would take hours and hours to water the entire garden this way. And the soil was so dry that it drank up the water quickly and still needed more. It was futile, she knew. Yet she kept at it, filling the bucket again and again and pouring it on the earth, until every part of her body ached and the daylight began to dim. Violet would bring supper soon and would be looking for her. She should go back upstairs. Dropping to her knees, she put her ear to the ground and listened. The silence lasted so long that she began to feel sick, worried that somehow she had done more harm than good. Then she heard it. The sound was as faint as before, but still there. She smiled with relief, but the very next moment she sat up in alarm. Something was in the garden with her. She had seen it move—just a quick flash in her peripheral vision, a shadow gliding up the slope toward the boulder. It had been too large and shaped all wrong to have been the black squirrel.

Roo got to her feet and stared all around her. Nothing moved. The garden was perfectly still and so quiet she could hear her own breath. Yet, she *felt* something was there with her. Watching. The way she had watched others from her own hiding places.

Chapter 13

"It looks like the Burrows will have to live without you for a while longer," Violet said when she brought in breakfast the next morning.

"What do you mean?" Roo sat up in bed, squinting against the sunlight as Violet pulled back the curtains.

"Phillip threw a fit when he heard you were leaving," Violet said. "He's threatened to have us both fired if you go. Ms. Valentine's not too pleased about it, I can tell you."

"What does he want with me?" Roo asked, too baffled to feel the full impact of the reprieve.

Violet shrugged. "Who knows? He's the most changeable person I've ever met. In any case, he's your ticket to stay here—though I can't imagine why you'd want to. If I were you, though, I'd try and be nice to him. He'll change his mind in a blink if you make him mad."

Violet stared hard at Roo for a moment, cocking her head to one side.

"What?" Roo asked, frowning.

"You have the greenest eyes, don't you? I don't know why I never noticed before. It seems like they've gone greener though. And you've filled out too. Do you know what my mother would say about you?"

Roo shook her head.

"She'd say, 'That girl's got a bloom on her.' Bah, don't look at me like that! It's a good thing! It means you're shaping up to be nice looking."

Roo scowled at this. "I know what I look like."

"Do you? Next time you pass a mirror, take a good long look in it. You might just surprise yourself. Now go on. Eat your breakfast and get dressed. Your cousin wants to see you this morning. Don't ruffle his feathers if you can help it."

Phillip was still in bed when Roo came to his room, using the east wing hallway this time, rather than the secret passage. He looked paler than he had the day before, but he smiled when he saw her. It was a nice smile too, Roo couldn't help but think.

"Sit down," he said, nodding toward the edge of his bed. They sat in silence for a while.

"Do you to want to play canasta again?" Roo asked finally.

"I'm not in the mood," he said.

"Fine," Roo replied.

She stuffed her hands beneath her legs and rolled her eyes. Let Phillip be difficult. It didn't matter. She was going to stay at Cough Rock. She could tend her garden and maybe even see Jack again, and if Phillip wanted to act like a brat, she would simply ignore him.

"What are you thinking about?" he demanded.

Roo shifted on the bed. "I don't know. Nothing."

Phillip frowned down at his thick blankets, then rearranged them fitfully.

Roo sighed and decided it would be in her best interest to at least try not to upset him.

"I was thinking about Jack," she said, not wanting to mention the garden.

"Who's *Jack*?" He said the name in a contemptuous way that made Roo want to slap him. But she took a breath and tried to keep her voice even.

"He lives on the water. Hasn't Violet told you about him?"

Phillip shook his head.

So Roo told him all the stories that Violet had told her, and to her surprise Phillip seemed just as riveted as she had been when she first heard them.

"Have you met him?" Phillip asked.

"Once."

"Did you like him?"

"Yes."

"More than you like me." Phillip said this as a statement of fact, and of course it was true.

She didn't want to provoke him though, so she quickly changed the subject.

"What's that song I keep hearing you humming?" she asked.

"I don't hum songs," he said testily.

"Yes, you do," Roo said, her patience failing.

"They're not *songs*."

"Well, I heard you humming *something*."

Phillip let out an exasperated breath, but Roo kept her eyes on him, waiting for an answer.

"It's just a thing my mother used to do, if you must know," Phillip said.

"Hum?"

"It was a special sort of humming. I can't do it the way she did. I try, but it's all wrong. She said it was something the mothers in her village used to do. It was supposed to make the children grow up strong. She told me all kinds of stories about the jungle. About jaguars and macaws and spirits that live inside every tree and every plant. She told me about these vines that wrap themselves around trees, all the way to the top."

Roo nodded. She knew those vines. The garden was covered with them.

"They're called lianas," he said. "She told me that they're the tongues of jungle spirits, and if you want to summon someone, you hold the end of a liana on a treetop and call out the person's name three times. They have to come if you do that, no matter where they are. She talked about the jungle all the time. My father built her a garden, here in the house, and he filled it with plants and flowers and trees from the rain forest. My mother and I used to spend hours there, playing and climbing trees and vines and splashing around in the water. You've never seen a more beautiful garden in your life."

While he spoke, Roo didn't move; she hardly breathed, afraid she would do something that might give away her secret.

"What happened to it?" Roo asked quietly.

"My father destroyed it," Phillip said, his voice turning dark. "After she died, he tore the whole garden out and walled it up."

He doesn't know, Roo thought with relief.

"Why did he do it?" Roo asked, remembering what Mrs. Wixton had said about people thinking Ana had been murdered.

"I asked him once," Phillip said. "He said something bad had happened there, and he hated to think about it. But that was all he'd say."

Phillip shifted in his bed, and suddenly looked at Roo intently. "If I tell you something," he said, "will you keep it a secret?"

"Okay."

"You promise?" he persisted.

"I just said I would, didn't I?"

"The first time I heard you behind that door," Phillip said, his eyes darting toward the door that led to the passageway, "I thought it was my mother."

"But she's dead."

Phillip's gaze returned to Roo. There was a damp, feverish look in his eyes that Roo found unsettling.

"She's still here," he said. "She's still in this house. I hear her."

The words, spoken with such gravity in the darkened room, spooked Roo. But she quickly collected herself and replied tersely, "I don't believe in ghosts."

"My mother said the jungle was full of them."

"She was just telling you stories," Roo said.

"No, she wasn't," he protested.

"Then she was silly and superstitious."

"Shut up! What do you know anyway? You're just a thief! I heard Ms. Valentine and Violet arguing about you this morning. Ms. Valentine said that you were a thief. She said your foster mother warned her that you stole things."

Roo felt her own anger rear up and she drew back to slap him; but at the very last second she thought about the garden. She took a breath. Her body shook with the effort to control herself, but she stood up.

"Where are you going?" Phillip demanded.

"I'll be back," she muttered, heading toward the doorway that led to the passageway.

"No! You're lying! Where are you going?" He began to shriek again, but she turned on him now, her face full of fury, and warned, "If you start shrieking again I won't come back at all."

This stopped him, and he managed to keep his temper until Roo returned a few minutes later, holding something in her fist. She tossed it on the bed.

"It's yours," she said.

Phillip picked it up and turned it this way and that. "A metatarsal," he said. "A coyote metatarsal." He looked up at her. "But where did you get it?"

"I stole it."

Phillip eyed her suspiciously. "Why are you giving it back?"

"So that the coyote won't limp."

Chapter 14

After she left Phillip, Roo spent the rest of the morning in the garden. The black squirrel watched from his perch on the tree as Roo carried buckets of river water into the garden and spilled it out onto the earth. It was lovely to see the parched soil drink up the water, but it was never enough. It had gone thirsty for too long.

As she worked, her mind kept wandering back to Phillip. He would want to see the garden again, she knew. He would want to know that it hadn't been completely destroyed after all. But each time she had nearly convinced herself that she should tell him, another part of her argued vociferously against it. If she did tell him, no doubt he would go and tell Violet or Ms. Valentine or his father, and then the garden would be shut off forever and left to die.

Roo had been thinking so deeply about this while filling her bucket by the river that she didn't see the canoe until it was right in front of her, bouncing lightly in the shallows. In the daylight she saw that Jack's hair was such a pale blond it was nearly silver where the sun hit it, but his skin was tan and his cheeks were ruddy. His clothes were strangely formal—black dress pants and an untucked button-down white dress shirt—but they were too big on him and tattered and dirty in places. His head was tilted to one side, watching Roo with quiet interest.

"Why are you staring at me like that?" Roo asked finally, glowering with discomfort.

"You look different," he answered.

Roo felt her gut pinch. She suddenly remembered that he'd seen her only from a distance and at night. Now that he saw her up close, in the light of day, he would realize how plain she was. It hurt her feelings, but still she answered defiantly, "This *is* what I look like."

He maneuvered the canoe close to the rocks, plunging his paddle into the shallow water to hold it still.

"Do you want to come for a ride?" he asked.

"I'm busy."

Jack glanced at her bucket, and then back at her. "The water will still be in the river when you get back."

Thoughts of the Faigne crept into Roo's mind. What had Violet said? That the Faigne was a water creature, not human at all. That was silly, of course, she told herself. He was just a boy. But still, when she looked at him she found that his beauty was almost otherworldly.

"I can't swim," Roo said.

"You won't have to," he replied.

Roo stared uncertainly at the little canoe. "Will it hold two people? What if I sink it?"

He laughed. "You don't weigh more than a rabbit."

He stretched out his hand and kept it there, waiting until she made her decision. After a few moments' deliberation, she put the bucket down and stepped across the rocks. Leaning over, she took Jack's hand. He steadied her as she stepped into the canoe.

"Bend your legs," he told her when the canoe began to rock. She shifted her body until the rocking settled, and then sat down opposite Jack. The sun had squeezed his pupils into pinpricks. His irises looked so unnaturally gray that Roo once again found herself thinking of the Faigne. But then the canoe slid away from the shore, putting the sun behind them, and his eyes looked more human again.

At first, Roo gripped the edges of the canoe, her heart lurching every time they hit a wave. But it wasn't long before she felt her body adjust to the motion. The little canoe rode the river lightly, rearing and dipping while Jack deftly maneuvered it. The water seemed to be grabbing the paddle at each stroke, passing the canoe hand to hand over its surface.

There were other boats on the river, though Jack avoided coming too close to these. Once, though, a fisherman spotted them. He stood up in his boat and shielded his eyes against the sun to see them better.

Tonight he'll tell his friends that he saw the Faigne, thought Roo, *and that a strange girl was with him. Maybe they'll think I'm a sea creature too.* Roo smiled.

Suddenly a long, loping shadow appeared above them. Roo looked up to see the white belly of a heron, its slender legs stretched behind it and its neck folded back against its shoulders. Roo expected the bird to pass on by, but instead it seemed to hover over them, keeping pace with the canoe. Now and then it would fly ahead of them and circle back, finally disappearing altogether when a large freighter trudged through the seaway.

"It's almost like that bird was following us," Roo said.

"He was. That's Sir."

"He's *yours*?" Roo asked, amazed.

Jack laughed. "I'm *his*," he said. "He's adopted me. He stays with me through the winter, even though almost all the other herons go south. He knows everything that happens on this river. He even told me when *you* first arrived here."

Roo shot him a doubtful look. But then she remembered seeing the heron that flew over the Boston Whaler on her way to Cough Rock, and how Ms. Valentine had said it was odd to see the bird at that time of year.

On and on they went, past stretches of polished shoal, peppered with cormorants; weaving around islands, some with homely cottages and others with gigantic mansions. The beauty of the St. Lawrence was staggering. Great green knolls rose up out of the water, like a relief map come to life, forming complicated labyrinths. The canoe skirted by a tremendous cliff made of red-veined rock. Jack pointed out a raven's nest on the cliff, but even Roo's sharp eyes could not make it out. Jack lifted his chin and let out a low, croaking sound and a shiny black bird emerged magically from one of the fissures. She croaked in response, staring down at them as they passed.

Finally they came to a narrow channel between two of the larger islands. Jack rowed to the top of the channel, then lifted his paddle out of the water.

"What are you doing?" Roo asked nervously.

Jack didn't answer. He just stretched out his legs and leaned back a little. The canoe bobbled in place for a moment. Then something seemed to seize it and the next second they were shooting down the channel. The little canoe vaulted over waves, then pitched down again at breathless speed. To Roo's surprise, she wasn't frightened at all. In fact, it made her laugh out loud, which seemed to delight Jack. The water sounded like it was laughing too—the muted, trilling sound of someone laughing in a rainstorm. Then suddenly it was over. The canoe slowed. Jack put out his paddle again and began to row.

"What was that?" Roo asked, catching her breath and smiling.

"Dumbfounder's Current. It sucks you in and spits you straight to the other side."

"The river sounded like it was laughing," Roo said.

"It was." He looked at her thoughtfully for a moment, then said, "I think I know why you look so different."

Roo's smile dissolved.

"Why?" She eyed him warily.

"You're not fighting the wind anymore," Jack said.

Roo frowned. "I don't know what you mean," she said.

Jack tucked his head down and hunched his shoulders slightly . . . and there it was. The same look she had always noticed in the mirror. The look of a thief. It bothered her that he had seen it too.

"So what do I look like now?" she asked.

"Like a girl who might capture a Faigne," he replied, smiling lightly.

She didn't know how to respond, so she turned away and fixed her eyes on a shoal covered with birds. The birds were small with soft gray bodies that tapered to white around their bellies. Their black masks scooped over their skulls, and their slender bills were the deepest red, tipped with black.

"What are they?" Roo asked, grateful to be able to change the subject.

"Terns. They're nesting."

Roo squinted against the sun and searched the shoal.

"But I don't see any nests," Roo said.

"That's because terns are terrible parents," Jack said, an unusual edge of irritation in his voice. "They put their nests any old place and don't even bother to make them well. Just a few twigs and leaves. Then the gulls come along and bully them, and off the terns fly, leaving their eggs for the gulls to eat or smash. Or sometimes the terns stick it out long enough for the eggs to hatch, but then the gulls swoop down and carry the chicks off. The adult terns barely even put up a fight." He turned his head suddenly and stared at a craggy section of the shoal.

"I see you," he whispered.

"Who is it?" Roo asked.

But Jack just held his finger to his lips. Spinning the canoe around, he began paddling close to the bank until he crept alongside a low outcropping by the shoal's edge. He leapt out, then held the canoe steady for Roo. She stepped onto the shoal and looked around, trying to find whoever had caught Jack's attention. All she saw were birds, though, scampering around in panic at the sight of them.

"This way," Jack whispered, and in a flash he was bounding easily across the rocks.

The shoal was wet and slick, and though she was naturally sure-footed, Roo slipped several times. Up ahead, Jack stopped abruptly. He held out his hand for Roo to stop too. Then he did the oddest thing. Shoving his hands in his pockets, his body seemed to go slack. He cocked one leg and his shoulders slumped. All his muscles seemed to loosen and relax. He stood like this for a moment, just as though he were waiting for a bus, before squatting down and smoothly scooping something up in his hands. When he stood, he was holding a slender, dark brown thing that squirmed in his grip like a fish.

"What is it?" Roo asked.

"Come look."

As Roo came closer she saw that the creature had already begun to settle down in Jack's hands. Now she could see that it had damp, sleek fur and a pointed, ferretlike snout. Jack brought the snout close to his face.

"I'm on to you," he said to the animal.

"Won't he bite you?" Roo said.

"She," he corrected. "And she won't. We're old friends."

He loosened his grip, and the lithe animal crawled up Jack's arm and settled on his shoulder.

"She's a mink," Jack said. "And a pig for tern eggs. I keep taking her off the shoal, but she keeps swimming back. I'll find a smashed shell on the rocks, the insides gone, and there she is, skulking away. Between the gulls and this one, it's pretty bleak for the tern eggs. I patrol this shoal a few times a day. It's sort of hopeless. But still, I can't help myself, you know?"

She *did* know! Before she could stop herself, Roo blurted out, "I found a garden. It's been kept a secret for so long that everything in it is dead. I've been watering it and watering it, but it's so big, and it's so hot in there that the soil doesn't stay damp for long. I can't keep up, but how can I stop? It's like you and the tern eggs."

Jack nodded. He thought for a moment.

"The garden must have a sprinkler system, though," he said.

"There's a panel of switches and timers in the basement. That might be for the sprinklers, but all the wires are cut. I think my uncle must have done it." And she told him what Phillip had said about the garden and his mother's death. Jack listened carefully. The mink took the opportunity to scamper down his arm and try to escape, but Jack caught her and held her to his chest.

"If you want," Jack said when she was finished, "I could help you. The garden might stand a better chance if there were two of us working in it."

When Roo hesitated, Jack lowered his head and whispered to the mink, "She doesn't trust me."

It made Roo smile.

"I do," she said. "I think I do."

They took the mink to a wooded island far from the tern's nesting place. Clearly it was a ride the mink had taken often. She stayed by Jack's feet in the canoe, occasionally stretching herself out across his shoes. Once she even approached Roo, nuzzling at her ankles. Roo kept perfectly still, delighted, her eyes darting between Jack and the mink. Slowly, very slowly, Roo bent down and with the tip of her forefinger she touched the mink's silky head. The mink tensed for a second, but when she didn't dart away, Roo let her finger slide down the mink's neck and along her back.

"You're good with animals," Jack said, surprised.

Roo nodded. "I'm just not good with people."

As Jack neared the shore, the mink seemed to know when they had arrived at her new home. She leapt onto his seat and then dove off the edge of the canoe. She swam the short distance to the bank and scrambled onto land, her wet coat now inky black, and then disappeared into the woods.

"Do you think she'll go back to the shoal?" Roo asked.

"I know she will. But so will I."

They had only been gone for a little over an hour, but when they returned to Cough Rock, a faint rosy light was already simmering in the sky beneath the blue. By dusk it would burn flamingo pink, and then night would shut it down completely and the stars would push through. There had never been skies like this in Limpette. For the first time in her life, Roo felt at home in the bigness of things; in the river that she could not see the end of and the sky that held both stars and herons.

Jack wedged his paddle in the shallow rocks, and Roo leapt out before he could offer her a hand.

"Now she's jumping off canoes like a mink," he said.

"Like a rat," Roo corrected. "Like a River Rat."

Chapter 15

The screaming started in the middle of the night. The long eventful day had plunged Roo into a deep sleep, and the screaming had wormed its way into her dreams as a shrieking red bird caught in a tremendous, ropy spiderweb. The bird twisted and thrashed, struggling to free itself from the web's hold without success. When a giant spider began to climb up the web toward the bird, the screaming became unbearable and Roo woke with a gasp.

Standing over her bed was Ms. Valentine, barefoot and dressed in a robe that hung askew. It seemed as if she too had woken suddenly. Her face, scrubbed of makeup, was tinged pink around the rims of her eyes and the wings of her nostrils, and her dark hair was disheveled.

"Get up, Roo," she said. It was less an order than a plea.

That was when Roo realized the screaming was real and not just in her dreams. It pierced the walls, hysterical and ragged, and was accompanied by a furious thumping.

"What's he screaming about now?" Roo grumbled.

"This is the worst we've ever seen him," Ms. Valentine said. To Roo's amazement she actually sounded frightened. "He's punching the walls, just . . . wild. Violet can hardly restrain him. Please, can you see what you can do—"

Roo groaned, but she got out of bed and started down the stairs. The screaming pounded through the house, echoing off the walls. It made Roo mad to hear it. She began to run, anxious to make it stop. The shrieks grew more and more hysterical, so that by the time Roo flung open Phillip's door, her face was flushed with her own fury.

Tangled in sheets and blankets, Phillip was screaming and tossing in his bed while Violet attempted to hold him down. When she lost her grip on one of his hands, it flew to her face and clawed at it.

"Stop it!" Roo screamed at him. "Stop it right now!"

But the attack did not let up—Phillip seemed beyond hearing—and he slapped at Violet as she tried to grab hold of his wrist again. Enraged, Roo ran across the room, grabbed the Gila monster from the shelf and threw it against the wall as hard as she could. It made an awful cracking sound and the bones clattered to the ground.

"That's one!" Roo called to him. "If you don't stop screaming, I'll smash them all!"

"No, Roo!" Violet cried. "You'll make him worse." Her face was badly scratched and her lower lip was bleeding.

"I hate you!" Roo shrieked at Phillip.

She picked up another skeleton and smashed it. Then another and another until finally she realized that the screaming had stopped. The only noise left was the cracking of bones and her own cries of rage.

She looked over at the bed. Phillip now lay quietly in Violet's arms, and they were both watching her, shocked, their faces still damp with perspiration from their struggle.

The door opened and Ms. Valentine stood at the threshold. For a moment she was silent, aghast at the wreckage of bones strewn across the floor, with Roo in the center of it.

"What have you done?" she demanded of Roo.

"She's stopped him, is what," Violet said, tipping her head toward Phillip. He was pale and his eyes were glassy but he was calm.

Violet settled Phillip back into bed. He lay as docile as an infant, as she untangled and straightened the sheets and blankets and arranged them neatly over him. It infuriated Roo that Violet could be so kind to him after what he'd done. The scratches on her face were raised and pink now, and blood had dried on her lip, forming a small, dark blotch.

"Shut your eyes," Violet crooned at him. He shut them obediently, but when she stood up to leave, he opened them again.

"Roo will stay," he murmured.

"Of course she will," Ms. Valentine said stiffly.

"No, I won't," Roo said.

Ms. Valentine shot a warning glance at her.

"I don't care. I won't," Roo insisted. "He's repulsive."

"He can't help it when he gets into fits like this," Violet said gently.

"He can help it!" Roo said. "He's just used to doing whatever he likes."

Phillip was watching her from his bed, and now she glared at him.

"You *can* help it," she insisted to him, her voice raw. They stared at each other for a moment. Phillip looked away, then back at her.

"Please stay," he said.

"There," Violet said, getting up and walking over to Roo to give her shoulder a squeeze. "That's as nice as anyone could ask."

She guided Roo over to the bed, and Roo let her, but she would not sit down next to Phillip. Arms crossed against her chest, she stood there as Violet and Ms. Valentine left the room.

"Are you cold?" Phillip asked. "You look cold in that nightgown."

"I'm fine," she replied stonily.

"Here." With some difficulty he peeled back one of the covers. "Put this around you."

It was the way he struggled to maneuver the blanket—so weak and fumbling. It made her feel a little less furious at him. She reached out and snatched the blanket, wrapping it around her shoulders—she *was* cold in the thin nightgown.

"Why did you hurt Violet?" she asked him, her voice still harsh.

"Why do you care so much about *her*?" he said, suddenly peevish.

"Why does she care so much about *you*?" Roo shot back.

"Because my father feels guilty, so he pays people to care about me," Phillip said.

"Violet would be nice to you no matter what," Roo insisted. "That's just how she is. And anyway, what does your father have to feel guilty about?"

After a moment, he said, "Because he can't stand to be around me. That's why he's never here. He really only wanted my mother, not me, and now that she's gone, he hires people to be with me since he doesn't want to."

Roo would have liked to contradict this. She would have liked to accuse her cousin of feeling sorry for himself. Yet she couldn't help but admit that it might be true.

"Well, maybe if you didn't bite him, he'd want to be around you more," Roo countered.

"He deserved it," Phillip said, his expression hardening.

"Why?"

"He told me he might send me away to Dr. Oulette's clinic in Rochester. He said that I would have to live there while they treated me for depression."

"Maybe it would be a good thing," Roo said.

"It would be a terrible thing!" Phillip pulled his legs up and wrapped his arms around them like he was already trying to root himself in the room. "*She* won't be at some clinic!"

"Who won't?"

"My mother."

"Phillip—"

"I know what you think. You think I'm crazy. So does my father. Violet says that I'm dreaming when I hear her, but it's not a dream and I'm not crazy. I hear her calling for me through the walls. I heard her tonight, clearer than ever."

Roo opened her mouth to tell him that his mother was gone, just like her father was. But then she remembered when she had first seen her uncle; how he had looked so much like her father, she thought it was him—though it made no sense—and how her whole body had filled with happiness at the sight of him.

"Lie back on your pillow," she told him, and sat beside him.

"Why?"

"Just do it," she said.

Once he lay back, Roo started, "There once was a little red-and-yellow boat called *Pendragon*—"

"I don't want to hear stories," he complained.

"Shut up," Roo said. "And instead of sailing in the water it flew above the treetops in the sky."

She told him the story about when Vincent landed on

the island of Malta, and after some initial squirming Phillip lay still and listened. Before long he closed his eyes. His breathing gradually slowed, and when she stopped talking to check, she saw that her cousin had fallen asleep. She pulled the cover up over his shoulders. He turned toward her in his sleep, and tucked his legs up. For a while she stared at him. Sleep softened his face. It was a solemn face, like her own. She reached out and lightly touched his hair, so dark and thick. Like his mother's hair, she guessed.

The door opened a crack and Violet peered into the room. She glanced between Phillip and Roo, shaking her head in wonder.

"Well, look at this," she whispered. "Two waves, smooth as glass. An old Donkey granny could sail across the two of you in a pie pan and never feel a bump."

Chapter 16

Roo spotted the heron first. He pushed through the pink and blue early-morning sky then circled back and disappeared behind the tall pines of a distant island.

He's coming, Roo thought. She felt the excitement climbing in her chest but sternly pushed it back down.

Don't be ridiculous, she told herself. *He's just a boy.*

A few moments later Jack's canoe appeared in the distance. The heron, Sir, flew above it. At one point Sir swooped so low that it seemed as if he were about to fly right into Jack. Roo ducked reflexively as Sir just cleared Jack's head, and Roo thought she could hear Jack laughing, although it might simply have been the call of a far-off gull.

As the canoe rounded an island and entered the seaway, heading toward Cough Rock, the currents seemed to push against it. Jack paddled and paddled but the going was slow. Roo paced along the rocks that formed a tiny cove, watching as Jack struggled against the river's mighty shoves. It seemed like he would never reach her. Sir, too, seemed to grow impatient. He flew to the canoe, landing awkwardly on its edge, and rested there while Jack paddled on.

It took nearly a half an hour for the canoe to fight its way to the island. As Jack maneuvered into the little cove, Roo reached out and grabbed the canoe to help pull it in. Jack's face was pink and damp with exertion as he stepped onto land, but he was laughing too.

"I think she's jealous," he said breathlessly.

"Who is?"

"The river," Jack replied. "Look at her, pretending not to notice us."

Roo looked at the water, flushed purple beneath the surface. Yes, the waves did hold themselves stiffly now, moving past briskly but occasionally serving Cough Rock with indignant little slaps.

He belongs to the river, Roo thought.

"Are you sure you want to do this?" she asked uncertainly.

"Of course I'm sure. Come on. Let's see your garden."

Roo led him over the rocks and around the back of the house to the basement door. At first she felt a rush of excitement at Jack seeing the garden. But as they climbed up the trapdoor stairs, she began to have misgivings. What if he thought the garden was hopeless? What if all he could see was a tumbledown graveyard of brittle, brown plants and dead trees?

At the top of the stairs she paused and looked down at him.

"Close your eyes," she ordered.

He closed them, and she scrambled up into the garden, and then squatted down beside the trapdoor.

"Okay, take another step up," she said.

He did. She had him take two more until his head was poking out of the trapdoor.

"Now give me your hand," she ordered.

He put out his hand and she took it. The skin felt rough and warm. She held his hand loosely, but his hand tightened around hers. She led him up the final stairs until he was standing inside the garden, his eyes still faithfully shut.

"Listen," she told him, "you have to love this garden. No matter what it looks like. Okay?"

"Okay," Jack said easily.

"It's not green like other gardens," she warned.

"I know. You told me. Can I open my eyes?"

Roo took a deep breath and released his hand. "Go on."

She watched as his eyes opened and he looked around. He took in the broken branches hanging off the trees, the limp foliage matted on the ground, the tangle of vines drooping from the treetops. After a moment, he began to wander through the garden, stopping to touch the trunk of a tree or reaching up to let his fingers brush against the tips of hanging vines. Roo stayed back and said nothing. She remembered how she had felt when she first saw the garden—the peculiar feeling of sadness and wonder.

"Do you think it has a chance?" she asked finally, her voice sounding rough to her own ears.

"It's hard to tell with wild things," Jack said, crouching down by the stump of a tree. "This winter I found a half-starved coyote pup. I took care of him till he started to look good and sturdy. It seemed like he'd be just fine. But then he died suddenly in the night. I don't know why. Then a week later, on Sawdust Island, I saw something strange hanging from the branch of a tree. Turned out it was a rabbit, all torn up. I figured a hawk had grabbed it and started flying off with it, then dropped it by accident. There wasn't much rabbit left. His leg was busted and his skin was ripped to shreds. I patched him up the best I could and figured he wouldn't make it through the day. But he did. And the next day he ate out of my hand and each day he got stronger until finally he was good as new, except he hopped sort of lopsided. It seems like there's something mysterious about what lives and what dies." He saw that Roo's face had gone grim, and he added, "But each time I find an animal that needs help, I help it as though I'm sure it *will* live."

So that is exactly what they did. All morning they worked hard, hauling buckets of water from the river. They found a pair of old rubber boots in the basement and they poked holes in the soles and used them as watering cans. Roo was getting stronger. She found she could hold fuller buckets of water and that she no longer tired so quickly. Again and again, she paused to check on the bare patches of soil, hoping to see something green appear, even though she knew it was silly, that it was too soon.

When they had finished watering the garden, Roo snuck some food out of the kitchen for their lunch. They ate beneath one of the dead trees—cheese sandwiches and purple grapes and a jug of lemonade. The black squirrel stopped by to ask for a bit of their lunch. Roo gave him some bread and he ate it at a distance of a few feet away, watching Jack circumspectly. Roo watched Jack too, noticing the way he ate, focused and silent, like a person used to eating alone.

"Don't you get lonely out on the river?" she asked.

Jack laughed. "How could I get lonely when the river never stops talking?"

"Lonely for people, I mean."

Jack took a bite of his sandwich and considered this, as though it were a new idea. "At night sounds carry across the water. I'll hear people talking and laughing. Sometimes I wonder how it would be to live like everyone else. I guess it would be nice for a while, but in the end I'd wind up running right back to the river. Honestly, I don't know how people can think without a river. Sometimes I'll be in my canoe, mulling things over, and my brain will leap right into the water and travel with it to where the perch are biting or where the raspberries just went ripe along the shore or to where there's a warm empty house. I don't know where *I* stop and the river *starts,* do you know what I mean? If we were separated, I think I would just . . . I would just unravel."

Suddenly, Jack's head whipped around toward the back of the garden.

"What is it?" she asked, following his gaze.

He didn't reply at first, while his gray eyes scanned the garden intently. After a minute, he looked back at her, his face perplexed.

"I thought I saw something," he said.

"The squirrel?"

Jack shook his head. "Definitely not the squirrel. It was a shadow. Up there." He pointed at the boulder. "It's gone now."

Roo bit her lip and hesitated before she confessed, "I saw it, too, the other day."

They were quiet, but they were both thinking of Ana because Jack suddenly said, "I saw her once when she was still alive, about four years ago."

"Where?" Roo asked.

"She was by the stone arch on Cough Rock, right at the spot where I first saw you. She had this long black hair and it was windy that day, so her hair was whipping all around. It reminded me of a flock of cormorants, just as they are about to take flight. She was pacing back and forth. Then he came out, your uncle, and he wrapped his arms around her and they went back inside." Jack looked at Roo, his eyes steady on hers, and said, "What if she's here? In her garden? Watching us?"

Roo thought of what Phillip had said, but she quickly shook this off.

"I don't believe in ghosts," Roo said.

"Really? That's funny. I believe in almost anything."

"He's crying for you."

Violet woke Roo in the very early hours of the morning. Even in the darkened room, Roo could see that her face was pinched tight with worry. "His heart is thumping so loud, you can hear it through the bedsheets."

Indeed, when Roo opened Phillip's door, she was shocked at how pitiful he looked. His head was thrown back against his pillow and his face was damp with sweat and tears. In a way it was worse than seeing him flailing around, slapping and clawing. Now he just looked ill.

Roo sat beside him on his bed, not knowing how to comfort him. For a while they sat together in silence. She tried to catch his eye but he would only look down at his blankets, which he twisted in his hands. Roo noticed that the veins on his thin hands were raised, like a snarl of electric cords.

"Tomorrow we can try and fix the skeletons I broke," Roo offered.

"I had Violet throw them all out," he replied.

Roo glanced over at the far end of the room. The shelves that had once been filled with skeletons were now bare. Even the coyote was gone, and the desk was cleared of glue and wire.

"But why?" Roo asked. Although she hadn't liked them, this seemed like a bad omen.

"I got tired of them," Phillip murmured, then looked away.

Roo sighed.

"You heard her again tonight, didn't you?" she said.

Phillip nodded.

"Maybe it was the river," Roo said. "Or the wind."

He pressed the heels of his hands against his eyes, then let them drop to the sides of his face. His dark eyes looked flat, deadened, like his father's eyes.

"Maybe," he conceded.

His quietness alarmed her. She wished he would scream and she could scream back at him. Instead, he turned over in bed with his back to her and tucked his legs to his chest.

"Do you want me to stay?" Roo asked. She watched one narrow shoulder rise and fall in a listless shrug.

Roo lay down beside him. It wasn't long before Phillip fell back to sleep, but Roo remained awake. She was turning things over in her mind, feeling the tug of a decision that she didn't want to make. She had found the garden, yes, but it wasn't hers. Not really. It was Ana's and so it was Phillip's too. Maybe Ana was waiting for him, down in the garden. Maybe the garden was waiting for him too.

Chapter 17

Dressed in regular clothes, Phillip looked even more fragile than he had in his pajamas. His spindly arms poked out of his short-sleeved shirt and a belt was cinched tightly around his pants.

"He won't like me," Phillip said.

"He might if you don't act like a monster," Roo replied. She reached over and adjusted his shirt collar so that his jutting collarbone didn't show.

"I don't see why he won't just come up here to meet me." His voice turned peevish.

"He's shy of people," Roo explained.

She had told Phillip only that she was going to take him to meet Jack. She hadn't mentioned the garden at all. Phillip's moods were so unpredictable that she worried he would throw a fit when he learned that the garden had been there all along, abandoned and left to die. It would be safer, she reasoned, for him to see it for himself, out of earshot.

"Do you remember what to say to Ms. Valentine?"

"I think so."

He pressed the buzzer on his nightstand. Ms. Valentine was at the door so quickly that Roo worried she had been just outside the whole time, listening. Her face revealed nothing, though, as Phillip gave her instructions: "I'm teaching Roo how to play chess today, and we are not to be disturbed."

"You're dressed," Ms. Valentine said with surprise.

"I *made* him get dressed," Roo cut in quickly. "I was sick of seeing him in his pajamas."

Ms. Valentine ignored her and studied Phillip's face. "Shouldn't you rest? You've had a difficult night."

"I'm fine," he said.

"Your eyes look a little bloodshot."

"My eyes are my business," he snapped at her. "Now leave us alone. If you bother us again, you'll make me mad, and I'll tell my father when he gets back."

Ms. Valentine hesitated, then glanced at Roo suspiciously before she left the room.

"She won't bother us now," he told Roo.

"I don't know how she doesn't hate you," Roo said, half marveling. "I would."

"My father pays her not to hate me," he said simply. He started for the door, but Roo stopped him.

"Not that way," she said. "We're going through here."

Roo led him through the door that opened out to the secret passageway, stopping by the chute. With the toe of her sneaker she gave it a little tap.

"That's our way down," she told him.

Phillip looked at the dark chute apprehensively. "I used to throw candy wrappers down it. Where does it go?"

"All the way to the basement."

Roo got down on the floor and went into the chute, feet first, careful this time to brace her legs against the edges to keep herself from sliding down. She looked up at Phillip. "Come on. I'll hold on to you."

Phillip crouched down and adjusted his legs so that they were resting over her shoulders. She wrapped her arms around his calves, then she pulled them both forward into the mouth of the chute.

"Ready?" she asked.

"I guess so," Phillip said, his voice faltering.

Relaxing her legs, Roo let herself slide with Phillip sliding behind her. When they began to pick up speed, Roo heard him make a small sound, as if he were trying to stifle a scream. Quickly she pressed her legs against the side again to stop them.

"All right up there?" she asked.

"Yes."

"You sound funny." She tried to twist her head to look up at him, but in that small space, it was close to impossible.

"It's just that . . . ," Phillip said, "it feels . . . I've never moved so fast."

"Do you want me slow down?"

"No. I want you to go faster."

Roo laughed, then wrapped her arms around his legs more tightly. "You asked for it."

She let go and they sped downward at full speed, their backs skimming across the cool metal. It was nearly as thrilling as Dumbfounder's Current, and the two of them laughed helplessly the whole way down, right up until they reached the bottom. And there was Jack, waiting there, looking bemused.

"It sounded like the walls were laughing," he said.

Roo shimmied to the floor so fast that Phillip slid onto the platform awkwardly, his legs strangely splayed. The smile left his face and his eyes darted toward Jack ruefully, as if he were waiting for an insult. But Jack had experience with creatures that were mistrustful of him.

"I'm Jack." He put out his hand for Phillip to shake. Phillip took it, and Jack gave him a discreet tug, just enough so that Phillip could ease himself into a sitting position and then slip off the platform.

His dignity recouped, Phillip now looked at Jack carefully, taking in the odd clothes, the pale hair in its short ponytail.

"Where is Sir?" Phillip asked.

"Just outside." Jack nodded his head toward the basement door.

"I'd like to see him," Phillip said, and started for the door, but Roo grabbed him by the wrist.

"Not yet. We wanted to show you something else first," she said.

She led him past the wired panel and he followed her up the narrow stairs with Jack behind him. Roo pushed open the trapdoor and they all scrambled up into the garden.

"It's still here," Phillip murmured as he looked around.

Roo braced herself for an outburst. Jack moved up beside him, hands in his pocket, his body looking deliberately relaxed.

He's trying to keep him calm, Roo realized. Like he did with the mink on the shoal.

But the crying and shrieking that Roo had expected never came. Instead, Phillip began to walk through the garden, looking up at the towering trees and the lacy brown creepers clinging to the glass panes; at the bare patches of earth and the small hummocks of leaf litter that Roo and Jack had piled in the corner.

"It used to be all green," he said finally, "with flowers everywhere."

He stepped onto the stone path and began to walk along it. "This was a stream."

"We thought it was a footpath," Roo said.

"No, a stream . . . there were berry bushes that grew along here." He paused to run his hands over a skeletal bush, then followed the stream to its end at the base of the rocky ledge, below the boulder. Gazing up, he said,

"And this was where the waterfall was. There are pipes in the stones."

"I didn't see them," Roo said.

"They're hidden. Look." He hopped out of the streambed and scrambled up the slope, his spidery body clambering over the rocks. When he got to the top, he pointed to the tiny metal pipes embedded in the stone. He showed them other things too, like the fissures in the rocks where flowers grew from and where the banana tree once stood, parsing it all out, just as he'd done with his skeletons. And in a way, Roo thought, all that was left of the garden was its bones—and a bat squeak of life beneath the soil.

Phillip stopped talking suddenly. His head lifted as though he were listening. Then he turned to them, smiling. A small, quiet smile of relief.

"What is it?" Roo asked.

"She's here," he said.

They found another bucket for Phillip, though he wasn't strong enough to carry it full. At first, Sir startled at the sight of Phillip. He spread his wings and scrambled into the air, flying to a nearby tree. But soon he grew used to him. As the stately bird patrolled the shallow waters for fish, he ventured closer. Once, Phillip reached out very quickly and let his fingertips brush against the bird's wing while Sir kept perfectly still, his round yellow eyes fixed on Jack.

After an hour of watering, Phillip grew tired. He stretched out on the boulder above the waterfall and rested his head on his flung-out arm while Roo and Jack kept working. Soon he lay so still that Roo went up to the boulder to check on him. Phillip's body had shifted so that it fit against the contours of the rock more comfortably. His right hip had found a depression to lean into and his right foot had slipped into a narrow crack in the lowest part of the rock. Roo put a hand to his cheek. His skin was cool and dry. He was breathing peacefully. Fast asleep.

Satisfied that he was okay, they left him so they could cool off in the river. They went down into the hidden cove and poured bucketfuls of water over each other's heads, while Sir paced the banks, watching them skeptically.

Even before they reentered the garden, Roo knew something was wrong. The door to the basement was slightly ajar, when she was sure she had shut it tightly. As she and Jack climbed the ladder to the trapdoor, a sickish feeling began to fill her belly.

"Someone's here," she whispered to Jack.

A shadow passed across the open trapdoor and they heard footsteps above them.

"Maybe Phillip's awake," Jack said.

Slowly Roo climbed to the top of the stairs and peered into the garden to see a pair of long, jean-clad legs.

"Oh, Roo," Violet murmured. She glanced over at Phillip, still asleep on the boulder. "What were you thinking?"

"He wanted to come," Roo cried. "He was happy. He was *laughing*! I've never heard him laugh like that."

"Yes, I heard him too. I heard the both of you, though for the life of me I couldn't figure out where the laughter was coming from. It was when I poked around outside and saw the trampled grass by the basement door that I put it together." Violet shook her head. "What have you done, Roo?"

"I've been trying to make things better."

"Better? What you've made is a colossal mess. Can't you see the harm you've done? Your uncle shut the garden up for a reason."

"What reason?" Roo countered combatively. "Because he killed his wife? Mrs. Wixton said people think he did."

"I know what people think, and I know the people who think it. They have all sorts of other nonsense to say too. If they had to mind their own business for a full week, they would give themselves hernias, every last one of them."

"Then why did he shut the garden up?" Roo demanded.

"I don't know. But that's not our concern, is it? What you should be concerned about is what will happen when your uncle comes back to find that you've opened the garden up and brought Phillip down here too . . . I wouldn't be surprised if he tossed us all out."

"Then you can't tell him," Jack said.

He had been hidden from Violet's view, behind Roo on the stairs. At the sound of this unfamiliar voice Violet's eyes narrowed.

"Who's with you?" she asked.

Roo said nothing, but an urgent tap on her back persuaded her to climb up into the garden so that Jack could do the same.

At the sight of him, Violet caught her breath. She looked at Roo, then at Jack, then back at Roo. "It *is* him, isn't it?"

Roo nodded.

Violet smiled, then put the back of her hand against her mouth as though to hide it. She shook her head. "If the Donkey grannies could see this . . ." Violet glanced back and forth at the two of them. "Even if I keep your secret—and I'm not saying I will—you'll be caught sooner or later. Ms. Valentine doesn't miss much. And if *she* doesn't guess, Phillip is bound to spill the beans during some tantrum. Incidentally, how were you planning to sneak Phillip back in the house?"

"I was going to wait until eleven when Ms. Valentine goes to Choke Cherry for the mail, and then tell you that Phillip wanted his lunch."

"And while I'm fixing it, you sneak him back upstairs."

Roo nodded.

"The nerve of you two!" But she seemed more amused than angry. Her eyes returned to Jack and she shook her head. "The Faigne, here in our house! The Donkey grannies would keel over! They'd never believe me, even if I swore up, down, and round the bend . . ."

Then Jack did the most astonishing thing. From his

back pocket he pulled out a knife and opened it. Grabbing the top of his ponytail, he sawed at the hair above the rubber band, and in a minute he held out his blond ponytail toward Violet.

"Show them this," Jack said. His hair was now short and jaggedy. It made him look more like a regular sort of boy—the kind that Roo might have seen on the streets in Limpette.

Violet stared down at the flaxen thing.

"Is this a bribe?" she asked, raising her eyebrow at Jack.

"Yes," he answered, smiling. And to Roo's relief, she could see the Faigne again in his smile, and so apparently did Violet.

"All right." Violet reached out and took the ponytail. "I'll keep your secret."

"Thank you, Violet," Roo said.

Violet nodded, her eyes still on Jack.

"You look real enough," she mused.

"You can squeeze me if you want," he said.

"Well then, I think I will." And she gave him a hug. When she let him go, she said, "Mind you, that was for my mother's sake. She thinks you're nothing but a boy who needs a home, and she'd plunk me on the head if I didn't say, Patty McPhail, Donkey Island, first house on the left on Quarry Street. Done."

With that, she walked up the garden's incline to fetch Phillip. But as she bent to wake him, she paused, her head tipped to one side as she stared at the boulder.

"How pretty," she said.

"What is?" Roo asked, hurrying over with Jack behind her.

"That little red flower," Violet said. "I didn't know flowers could grow on rocks like that."

Indeed, growing out of a narrow crack in the boulder, by Phillip's foot, was a spiky red flower where, Roo was quite sure, there hadn't been one before.

Chapter 18

Every morning, Roo and Phillip did schoolwork in Phillip's room, with Violet watching over. In her own way, she was as stern a teacher as Mrs. Wixton; but when the sound of Ms. Valentine's boat motor started up to make its mail run to Choke Cherry, Violet set them free. They hurried into the passageway and slid down the chute to the garden, though Violet said it was bad luck for live children to go down it.

The garden was changing slowly. One morning Roo noticed a patch of pale green near one of the walls of the atrium. To her delight she found several tiny new shoots, filament thin, pushing out of the earth.

"Look!" She called Jack and Phillip over to show them.

As they kneeled by the young shoots, marveling,

Roo stretched herself out against the ground and put her ear to the earth.

"What are you doing?" Phillip asked.

"Shhh," she told him.

The boys waited in silence as Roo listened.

"I can hear it," she said. "It's louder now."

"What is?" asked Phillip.

"The earth."

"You can hear the earth?" Jack asked.

"Of course. Can't you?"

Jack and Phillip shook their heads.

"That's funny," Roo said. "I thought everyone could."

"What does it sound like?" Phillip asked.

No one had ever asked her that before. She listened again. It was like a long fluttering sigh made between closed lips. It rose and fell in pitch, and there seemed to be a song woven through it that never repeated itself. Roo took a breath and tested out a sound. She stopped and shook her head.

"It's not exactly right," she said.

"Do that again," Phillip told her.

Roo gave it another try. She struggled to mimic the lilting rhythm, the way it snaked under and over itself.

When she stopped, Phillip was staring at her, his dark eyes so wide and bewildered that Roo sat up, alarmed.

"What's wrong?" she asked.

"That was how it sounded," he said. "Exactly how it sounded."

"What?"

"My mother's humming."

Day by day, the garden's ashy haze became interspersed with patches of fresh green. The first plants to bloom were the fragile shoots by the wall—with the most delicate yet complicated flowers Roo had ever seen. They had a slender bell-shaped center, ringed yellow on the inside, and lavender petals with gently fluted edges, like the sleeves of a small girl's nightgown.

Every day they found new things pushing out of the soil. It felt as if each new flower had convinced yet another one to bloom. Tall spikes of red flowers that looked like Aladdin's slippers attached to each other at the heel. Slender red-and-yellow flowers that flared out like torches and great papery white flowers with long necks that bent as elegantly as Sir's; and all around the boulder, forming a crooked wreath, spiked flowers of purple, blue, and yellow grew within the cracks. Bromeliads, Phillip called them. He knew what all the flowers were called, and as they bloomed he greeted them by name, like old friends—blue passion flower, goat's milk, parrot's tongue.

Other living things began to find their way into the garden too. Bees hovered over the flowers and ladybugs examined new leaves. Once they found a green snake—exactly like Roo's glass one—sunning itself on a rock.

"Yesterday, after you left, I noticed a little shoot growing up by the stump of one of the banana trees," Roo said one morning, as they were waiting for Jack to arrive. "Jack thinks it might be a new tree beginning to grow."

"Maybe the whole garden will be full of live trees one day, years and years from now," Phillip said.

Roo had never heard her cousin talk about the future before. She looked at him, noticing that he had lost that withered, pinched look. There was a new quickness in his eyes and the purple smudges beneath them had faded.

"It might," Roo said.

"How does it sound now?" Phillip asked.

"What?"

"The earth."

"I don't know," she said.

She got down on her belly and pressed her ear to the ground. She had never listened to a garden in full bloom before. There were layers of sound threading out in all directions.

"The whole garden is humming!" Roo cried. "The earth is humming to the seeds and the seeds are humming to the roots and the roots are humming to the leaves and each part is telling another part to stay alive."

One afternoon, after they had put it in a morning's work on the garden and Phillip was back in his room, Jack and Roo took the canoe out to see the terns' shoal. The snowy terns shrieked in protest as Roo and Jack approached the shoal, and others flew into the air and circled above them. Some of the nests had been plundered, with bits of shell littering the dried grass, but a few had clutches of beautiful brown-speckled eggs lying in the patchy nests.

"Who knows? Maybe some of them might make it," Jack said.

They checked the shoal for the mink, and when they were satisfied that she was not there, they hopped back into the canoe and headed for Cough Rock.

The day had been warm and clear, with thin-skinned clouds raking across the sky. But as they entered the seaway, the air suddenly cooled.

Jack tipped his head back and looked up at the sky.

"Storm's coming," he said.

Not a moment later a dark purple cloud swept in above them, low in the sky, and as it unfurled the rain began to fall. It was a hard, furious rain. It whipped the river into confusion. Jack began to paddle hard, though Roo could not imagine how he could see where he was going. A tricky vapor hovered just over the river's surface, and they sailed blindly into it. Each time the canoe pitched up, Roo sucked in her breath and held it until they crashed down again. She felt a rush of panic, certain that even if the frenzied water didn't flip the canoe, they would certainly ram it into an island or shoal. The canoe's bottom was filling—the tops of Roo's sneakers were underwater. Squinting to keep the driving rain out of her eyes, she looked at Jack. His expression was grim but focused on a shadowy mass a few yards in front of them. It might have been land but it was impossible to be sure. Still, Jack tried to paddle toward it, fighting the currents.

Each time the canoe was thrust aside by a wave, Jack maneuvered it back into line with the shadow, closer and closer until Roo was certain that it was an island. A wave sideswiped them and the canoe tilted so sharply that Roo let out a sharp yelp and a second later she felt the canoe's bottom rubbing against land. Quickly Jack leapt out and held the canoe while Roo scrambled out after him, her legs shaking so badly that she stumbled.

"You all right?" Jack called to her over the sound of the thrashing rain.

Roo nodded.

"Do you know where we are?" she asked as they carried the canoe onto the island and set it down on the bank.

"I have an idea. I'll tell you for sure in a minute," he said.

They headed into a thicket of woods that flanked the shore and rose high above the river on a sharp incline. The canopy of leaves helped shield them from the rain and muffled its roar. Bit by bit, Roo could feel her muscles unravel as they hiked up the hill, the smell of pine growing sharper as they went. Quite suddenly the trees gave way and they stepped out into a grassy clearing, in the center of which was a large red boat. It was such an unexpected sight—a boat roosting on top of a hill in the middle of the woods—that Roo stood in the rain, just staring at it.

"Come on!" Jack said, and they both ran toward the boat's set of makeshift stairs onto its deck and through a metal door that led inside.

"What is this place?" Roo asked, looking around at

the paneled walls painted bright yellow, the rows of slatted wood benches, and the wide windows with the arched tops. A hammock hung from the ceiling in the front of the ship, just behind the captain's wheel.

"It's an old tour boat," Jack said, collapsing into one of the bench seats. "No one's lived in it since forever."

"Do you stay here?" she asked, eyeing the hammock as she sat down on the bench in front of his.

"Sometimes. I'm careful though. Other people know about it too." He lay down on one of the benches, his head below the window, and put his hands behind his head. "Want to know my favorite thing about this place?"

"Okay."

"Lie down."

She lay down on her seat and turned her head to look at Jack. Between the slats she could see the top of his flaxen head, then his eyes, then his mouth with its scrolled upper lip.

"Now what?" she asked.

"Now look out the window," he said.

She twisted her head back a little to see out the arched window. The view was of the smoke-colored sky and, around the edges, the tops of the trees rocking in the wind. The dark clouds slowly slid past, making Roo feel like the boat was sailing in the opposite direction. Not sailing, really, but flying in the sky, just above the treetops.

Roo laughed.

"You see it?" he said, one delighted gray eye staring at her through the slat.

"Yes!" But she stopped laughing suddenly and sat up. "*Pendragon.*"

"What's *Pendragon*?" Jack sat up too.

"A flying boat. It's a story my father told me. The boat was red and yellow and it flew above the treetops. . . ." She stared at Jack.

"Do you think he was here?" he asked.

Roo imagined her father winding through the river in his skiff, restless, fearless. His pale eyes always searching for something new. He would have found this place somehow. In his own way he was as wild as Jack.

"I'm sure he was."

They both lay back down. Jack slipped his hand between a slat and held it out for her. She slid her hand out and took his, then turned back to the sky. The darkness was lifting. Bands of distilled sunlight were touching down on the wet pine needles, making them gleam silver.

"The rain's stopping," Roo said, turning back to Jack. He had been watching her, and now, caught, he blinked and his cheeks turned a deeper red. He looked upward at the thinning clouds.

"Not yet," he said. But it was unclear if he was talking to Roo or to the sky.

The wind shifted and a purple-gray cloud, thick and mottled, moved across the sky. The light inside the boat dimmed, and Roo and Jack watched as *Pendragon* flew back into the storm, its hull just clearing the tops of the trees.

Chapter 19

Late in the afternoon, the clouds began to thin, finally vanishing altogether. In their place was a placid blue sky. Heavy with rainwater, the river was dark and thick, and it moved so slowly that the little canoe had a quiet trip back. But as they approached Cough Rock, Roo lifted her chin and stared at the island with a quizzical look on her face.

The great house seemed to stand out awkwardly against the sky, and when the canoe angled around the island toward the cove she noticed that the Whaler was missing.

Something's happened, she thought.

Jack stopped paddling and tipped his head to the side, watching her carefully.

"Are you okay?" he asked.

At the sound of his voice, the dark feeling left. She smiled at him and nodded. But once she was inside the house, the apprehensive mood returned. She paused in the lobby, listening. The house was quiet, but that was not unusual. She sniffed the air, the way she used to when she found herself in uncertain situations. She smelled the scent of wood polish and damp air and beneath that something else too—a frenzied whipped-up residue.

She rushed across the lobby to the east wing and hurried up the stairs, then down the hall to Phillip's room, where she burst through the open door. The room was in chaos. The floor was strewn with books and games that appeared to have been flung from all the shelves, and in the center of it all was Violet kneeling on the ground. Her back was to Roo, though she turned at the sound of Roo's entrance. Roo thought that her eyes looked odd—pink and swollen. But Violet quickly looked away again and resumed picking up the pieces of a chess game. Roo watched in confusion as Violet carefully nestled each piece in the velvet-lined wooden box, twisting them so they faced outward.

"Where's Phillip?" Roo asked, her voice rigid.

Violet said nothing at first. Then, "I swear that man washes in with the storms."

"Who?" Roo asked. "*Where's Phillip?*"

"He's gone," she said. She put the last chess piece in the box, then shut the lid and snapped the latch. "Dr. Oulette's taken him."

Violet turned now and looked at Roo. Her eyes were

raw-lidded and bloodshot and she was clearly struggling to keep from crying again.

"Took him? Where?"

"To his clinic. In Rochester."

"And Ms. Valentine let him?" Roo cried, appalled.

"She had no choice, Roo."

"But Phillip was getting better," Roo protested.

"That's what Ms. Valentine told Mr. Fanshaw on the phone—even she saw it."

"Then why would he have sent Phillip away?" Roo asked.

"It was Dr. Oulette's doing. He's been pressuring Mr. Fanshaw to send Phillip to his clinic for months now. The biting incident nearly sealed it, but your uncle kept putting off the decision. Then Dr. Oulette showed up this afternoon. He checks in on Phillip every few weeks. I don't know what was said, but Phillip went into a rage. It was awful—as you can see." She waved her arm around the room. "So the doctor called Mr. Fanshaw, and Mr. Fanshaw told us to pack Phillip's bags, that he'd made his decision. He wouldn't budge on it, no matter what Ms. Valentine said. I even took the phone myself, snatched it right out of Ms. Valentine's hand, and I told him Phillip's change was nothing short of a miracle. He said miracles were nothing short of hogwash. And that was that. Well, you know how willful *Phillip* is, and where do you think he gets it from?"

"But if my uncle just came back, if he just *saw* Phillip—"

Violet shook her head. "He told Ms. Valentine that he won't be back in the States for another few months at least."

"But Phillip will be a wreck by then! He'll start wasting away just like before, worse than before because he'll be away from the garden!" Roo felt her throat clench. "I didn't even get to say good-bye to him."

"It's better that way, Roo. Really. It would have been worse for him if you were there, and it would have broken your heart. I nearly scooped him up and ran away with him myself, I felt so bad for him. My only consolation was that he scratched some lovely stripes into the doctor's face." Violet's brown eyes narrowed. "I hope they leave a scar."

The next morning the overcast sky turned the garden's ceiling panes into dusky gray diamonds. Jack would not come for another hour. He would be crushed too when he heard the news.

Roo watched as the black squirrel climbed up the garden's tallest tree, running along the ropy liana that coiled around it. He stopped, flipped himself around and stared down at her. It was just the same way he had looked on those stairs up to the trapdoor the first time she found the garden.

"I can't follow you up there," Roo said.

The squirrel turned and continued up the tree, higher and higher until he reached the very top. The uppermost tip of the liana hung off the highest limb. It was slender and tapered, bent like the tongue in the mask that hung in the east wing's lobby. It was right then that Roo remembered what Phillip's mother had told him about the liana. That they are the tongues of jungle spirits. And that if you want to summon someone, you hold the tip of a liana on a treetop and called the person's name three times and they have to come.

Roo walked up to the tree and looked at it speculatively. She was not afraid of heights, but she had never scaled a tree before; she had spent so much time finding places that were small and hidden, it never occurred to her to try it. This was a straight-up climb with few branches along the way, but the liana was so thick it formed a sort of rough ladder.

She put her hand on one of the coils and tested it. It was dry and hard, rough against her skin. She pulled herself up and wedged her foot on the edge of the vine. It held her weight easily, so she took another step upward. Bit by bit she climbed as the black squirrel watched her from above. When she was up high enough she found that she was able to see the river through the glass-dome roof, stretching out in all directions. It made her dizzy so she looked up again and focused on the tip of the liana.

The tree's trunk began to narrow, the branches growing precariously thin as she approached the top. The squirrel was perched on the branch just to her left, his eyes on her.

Almost there, almost there, she thought.

She grabbed the slender branch above her head. The

liana coiled around it like a snake, narrowing. The tongue-like tip quivered as she pulled herself up. Leaning her body across the branch, barely breathing, she stretched farther and farther until her fingers touched the end of the liana. She closed her hand around it and shut her eyes.

"Emmett Fanshaw, Emmett Fanshaw, Emmett Fanshaw."

Chapter 20

Mr. Fanshaw did not come home. One week passed. Then another. The sky turned hot and white. Outside the air grew thick and the sun beat down on the river so that it burned silver at midday. The fish plunged deeper in the water, trying to escape the heat.

In the garden, Jack and Roo continued to tend the newest green shoots. They grew more thickly every day. The weeds did too. Jack and Roo tugged at them day in and day out, though the heat in the garden bore down on them mercilessly. The soil could not drink enough. They had no sooner poured out their bucket loads than the earth turned ashen again.

"The flowers look feverish," Jack said.

Roo knew what he meant. Their colors were almost

too bright, like skin that was flushed. If the heat kept up, she doubted they could keep them alive.

Outside, Sir was croaking. He had staked out his hunting grounds by the cove, and now he often chased off ducks or loons that came too close, charging at them with his rasping call. But when the croaking didn't stop, Jack frowned.

"What is it?" Roo asked.

"I don't know." Jack started for the trapdoor, but it was too late. Ms. Valentine's head appeared, then her body. In a moment she was standing in the garden, her face pale with outrage, and beside her stood Mr. Fanshaw.

"What on earth do you think you're doing?" Ms. Valentine demanded.

Roo's attention was on her uncle though. His brow was cinched as his eyes drifted across the stretch of flowers blooming wildly everywhere.

"How is this possible?" he muttered.

"It's the girl," Ms. Valentine said. "I told you she has been a problem from the start. But this is beyond everything . . . I had no idea, Mr. Fanshaw." She glared at Roo and demanded, "Who is the boy there? How did he get into the house? Does Violet know what you've been up to? "

"You can go, Ms. Valentine," Mr. Fanshaw said. "Leave my bags in the boat, I'll get them later."

She left reluctantly, showering a withering look on both Roo and Jack before she went. For a moment, Mr.

Fanshaw stood quite still, looking at the flourishing blooms tumbling across the garden. Curling petals dripping from tall stems nudged against wild bursts of orange and purple threadlike petals that reached out like sea anemones. And rising up out of the waxy green leaves, growing in the soil and on the rocks, were the brilliant spiked flames of the flower that had grown by Phillip's foot. In her uncle's face Roo recognized the look of wonder mixed with something else, something more tangled.

"How did you do this?" he asked in a faraway voice. "The garden was dead."

"It was dying, but it wasn't dead," Roo told him.

"We watered it from the river," Jack said.

"Phillip helped," Roo added defiantly.

Mr. Fanshaw looked at her full-on, and once again Roo felt a lurch of emotion at how like her father he was. But then his expression hardened and her father vanished.

"You brought my *son* here? You had no right," he reproached. "I shut the garden up for a reason."

"For what reason?" Roo demanded.

"If you plan on living in this house, Roo, there's one thing you'll have to learn," he said coldly. "The Fanshaws are private people. We keep our troubles to ourselves."

"You keep things hidden. There's a difference," Roo shot back. "There were living things in this garden when you shut it up. You nearly killed them. And you've done the same thing to Phillip. You walled him up in this house, and now you've walled him up in some clinic! Everything is a secret here. Everything is hidden. I hate it! I don't blame my father for running away!"

Mr. Fanshaw flinched at this. Then he looked around the garden again, his eyes settling for a moment on the boulder.

"You want to know why I shut up the garden?" he said.

Roo nodded.

"I suppose he's told you the local gossip?" Mr. Fanshaw's eyes flitted toward Jack. "About how my wife died?"

"I heard it, but not from Jack."

"And do you believe it?" Mr. Fanshaw asked, as if he already knew the answer.

"No," Roo answered.

"Well, you should. The gossip is right. Right on the whole."

"What do you mean?" Roo asked.

"When I first saw Ana, she was sitting on a rock by a waterfall. I had gone in the waterfall to cool off, and when I came out, she was there, above me, watching. I've never felt easy around people, not like your father. But with Ana, it was different. It was effortless. She was—" He faltered, shook his head. "I couldn't believe she loved me too. But she also loved the jungle, and she left it to be with me. So I built her a garden. I brought in the best landscapers from all over the country and they filled the garden with the same trees and plants and flowers that grew by that waterfall, where I first met her. I wanted the garden to be a living poem to her. Everything needed to be exactly the same. I insisted on it. But there was one plant that the landscapers couldn't find—a type of bromeliad. It had a beautiful red bloom and had grown out of the rock that Ana was sitting on when I first saw her. The landscapers brought in plants that were like it, but they couldn't find the exact one. Ana said she didn't care, but I couldn't rest until it was perfect. That's how I'd always been. It was a point of pride for me. I went back to Brazil, back to the waterfall, and I found the plant. I hid it in a mask that was specially made with a false front and smuggled it back into the country—I was that obsessed—and I planted it there." He pointed to the boulder. "What I didn't know was that something was hidden in the plant. I found it later, after Ana became sick, when I realized what I should be looking for. A brown spider, very poisonous, hidden in the leaves. But it was already too late. Ana died just a week after the thing had bit her on the leg. I had the garden fumigated and then I shut it up. I just couldn't bear to look at it again. It reminded me that I had been the cause of her death. And Phillip . . ." He sighed and shook his head. "I took his mother from him. And I'm a poor substitute. I couldn't do anything to help him either, so I've just . . . stayed away."

"Then why did you come back here now?" Roo asked. "Why did you come into the garden?"

"For the past two weeks I kept seeing Ana everywhere. I would see her standing beside a tree or moving through a marketplace. I'd even hear her voice calling my name. But when I'd come close she was never there.

I had pushed her out of my mind for so long. Now it felt like she was insisting that I think of her, that I pay attention. I felt like she was calling me back to Cough Rock, back to her."

"Phillip thought he heard her too," Roo reminded him.

"I know. And now that I'm here, I think I was wrong. Ana wasn't calling me back to her at all. She was calling me back to Phillip."

Chapter 21

Draped across a branch, high up on the black squirrel's tree, Roo looked down at the lianas that canopied the greens and pinks and reds of the garden. The view reminded Roo of the Lucite domes of flowers she used to place around the crawlspace under the trailer. How funny to see things from above when she had spent so much of her life burrowing into things, watching people's feet pass by.

Down below she could see Phillip standing with his back pressed against the tall sheer rock, dressed only in shorts and no shirt. He was still thin but his shoulders were no longer hunched and his chest had filled out in the past few weeks. He was smiling and his eyes were squeezed shut as he called out, "Not yet!"

She turned away and looked through the garden's

domed glass roof. The St. Lawrence stretched in all directions, blue and burnished. Roo traced the white scars on the surface—one to a wooden boat, another, a frantic ringlet—to a Jet Ski. And then she saw what she was looking for: an angular gray-blue silhouette of a bird slicing through the sky, then circling back.

She climbed down the tree, using the thick, twisting lianas as steps. These days she scaled the tallest garden trees nimbly and with no fear. She passed the black squirrel on her way down just as he was climbing up. They glanced at each other quickly—the amiable greeting of two wild creatures with many things to do—then continued on their way.

There was a sudden loud hiss and Phillip yelled out, "It's working!"

Roo looked down to see a curtain of water tumbling over the top of the sheer rock, splashing down into the once-empty pool and coursing through the streambed, filling it. Phillip was completely concealed behind the waterfall, except for his arms, which poked through the falls and waved at Roo. She could hear him laughing and laughing, the way he had laughed when he slid down the chute.

In a moment she saw her uncle climb up into the garden from the trapdoor, smiling at the rush of water, and at his son behind the waterfall, and finally at Roo, who jumped down from the tree.

"Going in, Roo?" He nodded toward the waterfall.

She smiled and shook her head. "Later."

Outside, the day was clear and bright. She sat on the rocky ledge above the little cave where she had once hidden, and she watched the canoe approach the island. The river was unnaturally calm. Its surface was laid out like a fresh sheet snapped smooth, and the canoe slid across it effortlessly.

The sun caught on her silver ring and made it gleam white. Roo traced her finger over the two hearts. Had a friend of the girl from long-ago given it to her as a gift—the two hearts being each of them, fused together forever? On an impulse, Roo hopped off the ledge and scrambled into the cave. It had been so long since she'd been inside it. For a moment she remembered the comfort of crouching in tiny places and looking out at the world, watching it without being part of it. But it wasn't long before her legs felt cramped and she began to crave the movement of the air outside. With her pointer finger she dug a hole into the soil. Then she removed the ring from her finger, dropped it in the hole, and covered it over with earth before scrambling back outside.

"Where are you off to?" Violet called, half her body leaning out of the first-floor window.

"To visit the tern chicks," Roo called back.

"Good day for it," Violet said. "I've hardly ever seen the river this quiet. The Donkey grannies must have left Jack a very generous offering this morning."

The little canoe pulled up to the island. Jack steadied the canoe as Roo climbed in and raised the paddle in greeting toward Violet, flashing her a smile.

"Yes, yes, you're very charming! Just remember to bring her back to us," Violet called to him.

They skirted the islands, which seemed like old friends now. Roo knew the secret coves and the places where the deer swam from one island to another. She knew where a toppled pine served as a diving board for the ducks and where the crows had hidden their nests in the bluffs. Yet just when she thought she knew the St. Lawrence, the river showed her something new and mystifying. Just like Jack. Sometimes when they were in the garden she would look at him and wonder: *When the trees grow tall, years and years from now, will we still know each other? Or will you just drift away one day, like the ice floes during spring melt?*

"Hey." Jack stretched his legs out and captured her ankle between his bare feet and held it there. "What are you thinking about?"

"I'm thinking . . . I'm thinking that I might like to learn how to swim."

Jack's face brightened. "Really?"

Roo nodded.

"I'll teach you," Jack said. "You'll see. By the end of the summer, you'll be swimming like a dolphin."

Sir swooped down over them, then rose again and headed off toward Eel Bay to find some lunch. I think we'll go with him now. The day is so clear, we'll have a fine view of the islands below—green puzzle pieces flung across the water, waiting for someone to fit them back together again. If we follow Sir, we'll pass directly over

Cough Rock. Look down. There is the great stone house, so formidable even from above. You can see the garden's glass dome in its center, cradled like a secret jewel.

A huge flock of cormorants has gathered beneath the island's stone arch, stretching out their sleek black wings in the sun. It's a strange sight. Cormorants have never collected on Cough Rock before, and Sir circles back to get a better look. All at once the cormorants take flight. Their bodies rise in a single black mass that billows out and twists, undulating like a woman's long black mane of hair, whipping in the wind.

Acknowledgments

Sometimes it takes a village to write a book. In the case of *The Humming Room,* it was the village of Clayton, New York. I owe an enormous debt of gratitude to Star Carter, naturalist and Director of Land Conservation at Thousand Islands Land Trust, for connecting me to so many river folk, both human and otherwise. Thanks to Brian Parker, island mail carrier, who kindly let me hitch a ride on his green Starcraft. Thanks to the gracious Skip and Joan Tolette for introducing me to the beauty of Grindstone Island. Thanks are also due to Sue-Ryn Burns Hildebrand, wildlife rehabilitator and local heroine.

Many thanks to Neil Mattson, Assistant Professor of Horticulture at Cornell University, for his patient explanation of how an almost-dead garden could be resuscitated.

I am especially grateful to my editor, Jean Feiwel, who consistently knocks me out with her astute editorial suggestions and her faith in me. I appreciate it more than I can say. Thanks also to the wonderful Feiwel and Friends posse, Holly West, Rich Deas, and Jason Chan, whose cover art never fails to make me swoon with delight.

As always, I am forever and endlessly grateful to my extraordinary agent, Alice Tasman.

Special thanks to my dear friend Anne Mazer. This book could not have been written without her wise counsel. Thanks also to friends Megan Shull, Mollie Futterman, and Mary Waterman, and to my two favorite guys, Adam and Ian.

And of course, the greatest debt of gratitude belongs to Frances Hodgson Burnett, whose garden continues to bloom in readers' hearts one hundred years later.